Millicent's
Gift

ANN RINALDI

HarperCollinsPublishers

Millicent's Gift
Copyright © 2002 by Ann Rinaldi
All rights reserved. No part of this book may be used or reproduced in
any manner whatsoever without written permission except in the case
of brief quotations embodied in critical articles and reviews. Printed in
the United States of America. For information address HarperCollins
Children's Books, a division of HarperCollins Publishers, 1350 Avenue
of the Americas, New York, NY 10019.
www.harperchildrens.com

Library of Congress Cataloging-in-Publication Data
Rinaldi, Ann.
    Millicent's gift / by Ann Rinaldi.
        p.   cm.
    Summary: Like all her brothers and sisters, Millicent has received a special
gift from her magical family, but she quickly learns that a gift can also be a
burden.
    ISBN 0-06-029636-4 (alk. paper) — ISBN 0-06-029637-2 (lib. bdg. : alk.
paper)
    [1. Magic—Fiction. 2. Family Problems—Fiction. 3. Family life—Fiction.
4. Supernatural—Fiction.]—I. Title.
PZ7.R459 Mg 2002   2001039734
[Fic]—dc21   CIP
                                                                     AC

Typography by Amy Ryan
1 2 3 4 5 6 7 8 9 10
❖
First Edition

In memory of all my aunts,
who had their own forms of magic

Prologue

I have to study this book about Celtic mythology. My aunts insist. How else will I ever get certified to use my Power? My Gift?

It's special, this Gift, and all the women and some men in my family have it, and because I will turn fourteen in September, I'm coming to the end of my apprenticeship and will soon be able to use it.

It's simple, really. I have one wish that I can use any way I want in life. Of course, I have minor powers, too, which I've been training for—spells, out-of-body experiences, all kinds of psychic goodies.

This was handed down to us on Mom's side, which has been traced back to Lady Sybil of Bernshaw Tower in Lancashire, England, in the sixteenth century.

Don't think it's all fun and games, though. Before I am granted use of my Gift, I have to study hard: all about nature—which means not only herbs, but the spiritual and mystical powers of creatures—about astronomy, astrology, folklore, religions, the whole nine yards.

And this: I can't lie. Not ever, not for the last five years, since I've been in training. If I do, I'll lose my Power. Oh, I don't mean telling a friend that yeah, she looks great in a new sweater when she looks like a toad. That's a kindness. I mean, I can't lie to my mom about not having homework. I can't lie to my brother Mac when he asks if I was snotty to my aunt Melanie, who up until now has home-schooled me, and who's my Mentor in Magic.

My brother Mac is the guy I answer to in life. The Dispenser of Favors, the Giver of Allowances, the Taker of Privileges, the Keeper of Chivalry, the All-Seeing Eye. More about that later.

Anyway, not lying is the central element in my life. It causes me all kinds of problems. It's a big burden for somebody my age. You try it. And here's something else: Nobody has to know I lied for me to lose my Power. It just won't be there for me when I want it, is all.

Sometimes I wish I was normal, like everybody else my age. Believe me, this Gift is a drag. And as far as I can see, it's been nothing but, for everybody in my family.

This book on Celtic mythology isn't bad, though. In it are all the gods, goddesses, druids, warrior queens, knights, spirits, fairies, misshapen giants, maids of this and that, shamans, sorceresses, doomed sons, and bewitched daughters whose wrath was terrible and whose love was unending.

Also in it are otherworlds, castles, forests, hells, tombs, realms, isles, towers, and enchanted wildernesses that these people inhabit.

There's a lot to learn. But it has pictures, too, of all the heroes and heroines, and with each picture there's a thumbnail sketch.

That's what I want to do here. Introduce my family in

thumbnail sketches. Forget the pictures. Better you should form images of them in your own mind. Create your own vortex of energy swirling about them. Because my family has enough deep-rooted quarrels, fears, secrets, curses, quests, traumas, disappearing acts, clever tactics, bouts of temper, and charming personalities to fill a book of mythology all its own.

Okay, so nobody has a silver hand or drags around enormous clubs or gouges people's eyes out. Nobody locks anybody in a crystal tower or swallows a fly to become pregnant. Nobody eats babies or has a pack of hounds that fly around at night in pursuit of human souls.

My brother Mac has that dog of his, Finnian, but his fangs don't drip. He's only a K-9 dog, and he's getting old.

Aunt Melanie keeps birds and has a sign outside her house that says, "Caution, Owls in Flight." But nobody has a cauldron to drink from that'll keep us young forever. All we have is the river here in Glen Laurel that overflows when it rains too hard and cuts us off from the rest of the world.

We're just ordinary people trying to make it in ordinary times with the same problems everybody else has. The degree of our magical abilities is determined by the degree of belief we have in ourselves. And the perceptions others have about us.

Sure, Aunt Melanie can change herself into a swan or a deer or anything she wants. I have seen it with my own eyes.

Who do you think that white doe was that stopped traffic out on the highway last July 25, which was St. James's Day? Aunt Melanie. We don't venture much out there except for major shopping trips. It's the Outside, and we don't have much truck with it. But there she was, smack dab in the middle of the road.

Fish and Game, the Save the Wildlife nuts, everybody was there. And in the end it was Mac who got her with a tranquilizer gun. Mac, who won't have anything to do with magic.

The next day, Aunt Melanie had a big red spot on her shoulder that was fast turning blue. Nobody saw it, because she wears those draped dresses, even in summer. I told her to show it to Mac, but she wouldn't because of his attitude about magic.

But I'm getting distracted, scattering my energies. Give me a minute while I collect them. There. Now let's get to the thumbnail sketches.

I'm also going to give you some info on the people in Celtic mythology that I compare my family to. I call those people "Celtic Twins." I think everybody in my family is a throwback.

Then, once you meet my family, you can run for a nice safe haven, the first refuge you come to, even if it's an island divided into four kingdoms that are separated by rivers of blood. Or, you can continue reading.

Cast of Characters

ME: Millicent MacCool. I was born under a full moon at the exact moment of Mabon, also known as the Autumn Equinox, September 21. It is a time of equal day and night, so Aunt Melanie always tells me to use that as a lesson and learn to balance my normal life with my life of magic.

This is easier said than done. Besides, after this night, the days grow shorter. The sun begins to wane in power and the darkness takes over.

Aunt Melanie also says I have to work hard to keep the darkness from taking over in my life.

The Autumn Equinox represents two things: thanksgiving for the things you have, and a sense of purpose to hold on to them. I feel that way most of the time. I know what I've got, but I often feel it slipping away from me, and I want to hold on. Especially my Power. There isn't a day that goes by that somebody doesn't try to make me feel either guilty or selfish for having it.

The corn baba is the symbol of this time. It represents both thanksgiving and a sense of purpose. Every year around my birthday, I make one. Aunt Melanie taught me how. It's made from dried husks of the corn cob. You've probably seen them. They are called corn husk dolls. I hang mine above the door in my room, make a new one every year and burn the old one.

Aunt Melanie says don't worry, I'm going to do fine with my magic. She says I carry the essential distillation of the memories of all my ancestors in my DNA. And I really have a knack for it.

I have a twin brother, Dexter. We're fraternal twins, and though we stay out of each other's faces, we're on the same cosmic level lots of times. He's been to regular school all along.

Now I have to go to school, and I hate the whole idea of it. Who needs calculus? I can see a vortex of energy over people's heads. I can see what color their auras are. Gym? I have out-of-body experiences at night when I sleep.

I have one friend, Naomi Carlson. She's got a terrible home life. Her father's in prison. She lives in a ratty old house that hasn't seen a paintbrush in fifty years. But she has an appreciation for my problems, and what's brought us together is that we both have fathers who aren't around.

My daddy left when I was eight.

MY CELTIC TWIN: I think it's Morgan Le Fay. She was King Arthur's half sister and the mistress of Sir Accolon of Gaul. She plotted the downfall of King Arthur. And knowing my brother Mac, I can see why. But then, when Arthur got wounded in battle, she took him in a black boat to Avalon and nursed him back to health. I suppose I'd do the same for Mac if push came to shove.

MY MOM: Mehitable. She fell in love with my dad because he had auburn curls and broad shoulders and his name was MacCool, a name right from Celtic legend. She's an artist, an illustrator, only she hasn't made a sale in a long time and has her stuff at lots of publishing houses. To bring in extra money, she hand-paints cards that sell at local shops, and she decorates people's homes for the holidays. She also runs the haunted house in town every Halloween.

There's a stream running through our basement. When Dad rebuilt the house, she made him leave it there. She thinks it's magic water. The house is over two hundred years old and is haunted by an ironmonger who lived here during the Revolutionary War. He fixed muskets for the Americans. When he turned his coat and started giving those muskets to the British, he was hanged under a full moon. Mom is the only person in the family besides me who hears him banging away in the basement.

HER CELTIC TWIN: Blathnat, wife of King Cu Roi of Munster. She betrayed her husband's people by showing Cu Roi's enemy the way to enter her husband's fortress. A stream flowed through it. My mom, betraying her husband? Well, Dad thought so. That's why he left.

MY DAD: Frank. Mom called him Finn from the get-go, after Finn MacCool the Celtic hero. He was an orphan, brought up by the nuns. He has no patience with magic. He's a building contractor. And he doesn't see the magic in what he does. I do.

He was building some real expensive house for some new-money people in town when Mom discovered that the site bordered on an old Indian burial ground. The Indians' descendants (they were Delawares, I think) wouldn't let him continue. The house stands, half finished, jutting right out onto the river. I go there when I want to be alone. It's my own secret place.

7

When Dad left five years ago, he had papers drawn up that left my brother Mac in charge of Dexter and me. We don't know where Dad is, 'cause his company has building jobs all over the place. When he wants to see us, he tells Mac and we go to wherever he is.

His Celtic Twin: Finn MacCool, leader of the Fianna, the elite band of warriors who guarded the High King of Ireland. He was brought up in secret. He went into a deep sleep until Ireland needed his aid. He had a saying: "A man lives after his life, but not after his dishonor."

My oldest brother: Mac. Mackenzie MacCool. He was in the FBI, and he's now chief of police in Glen Laurel. Okay, to give the Devil his due, he's known as a stand-up guy, as well as a hands-on chief, which means he doesn't sit behind a desk all day, but goes out on the road and gets involved.

His friend in the FBI was killed when they were both in a firefight during a hostage situation. Mac hunted down the lowlife who killed his friend. They gave him some kind of an award and declared him to be a Force of Light or something. But he came home to Glen Laurel anyway, and he's got some secret, some underground stream of sadness in him that he doesn't talk about.

He has the same auburn curls that my dad had at that age and my dad's blue eyes, which are like the sun. Because sometimes you can't look right into them. He has a kind of square face and he doesn't talk much, but he's always watching and listening. And when he does talk, it's slow and quiet and you don't want to miss it because somehow you know you'll be the loser if you do.

He plays chess and he and Carol Mitchell, my piano teacher, were an item when I was about five. Then both married somebody else, Mac went into the FBI, and both got divorced. I think they still love each other.

Mac was given the Power, too, but he rejected it. Aunt Melanie says the world is black and white to Mac. No gray areas at all. A person is right or wrong. No excuses.

HIS CELTIC TWIN: Sir Owain, one of King Arthur's warriors. When a fellow knight was killed, Owain wounded the Black Knight, who did it. The Black Knight rode back to his castle. Owain followed and became a prisoner in its walls. When the Black Knight died of his wounds, Owain married his widow. Then King Arthur sent for him and he went back to court. Soon he was accused of unfaithfulness, and was so overcome with shame he went to live as a hermit till he got his head on straight and went back to live with his wife. (Oh yeah, happily ever after.)

AUNT MERCY: Lives with Aunt Melanie in the Victorian bed-and-breakfast they run. Mom's sisters. Both are divorced. Aunt Mercy is a certified nurse and midwife at the local hospital. She grows her own herbs in the back garden. She says her herbs are sacred. She's a good, decent lady and I'm lucky to have her as an aunt. She has helped with my training, especially with the herbs that have to do with magic.

HER CELTIC TWIN: Brigid, goddess of healing. She assisted women in labor and could feed animals without the food supply ever diminishing.

AUNT MELANIE: Her first husband was killed in Vietnam. She divorced the second one because he had allergies and she's obsessed with flowers. Her flower garden will knock your socks off. She's the one who has the sign outside about the owls. She can turn herself into different things, and she has the most beautiful eyes I've ever seen. She used to be a

9

teacher, which is why she was allowed to home-school me.

HER CELTIC TWIN: Emer, whose father was a chieftain. She married Cuchulainn, who said her eyes were wide and proud and brilliant, like his favorite falcon. She didn't want him to go and fight, but he went off anyway and was killed in battle.

MY SISTER: Martha. Dead. Yeah, she was about seven when she died of complications from chicken pox. It affected the whole family. There are pictures of her all over the house. She was a beautiful fairy child. Nobody ever talks about her.

MY OLDER SISTER: Madeleine. She's the most beautiful of all. She was ten when Martha died. She has always lived in her own dream world. She used her Power in high school to get Spencer Hurd to date her. He did and they married young. Spencer drank and died in a drunk driving accident in which he killed two others. Madeleine was in the car with him, but before the accident, she threw herself out of the car. Her face got pretty banged up, but the plastic surgeons did a great job on it. You can hardly tell. She wants everybody's sympathy for this. But she's such a pain in the butt that I think she drove him to drink. Her loyalties go with the wind and she's conniving, basically dishonest, and believes her own lies. She's a hairdresser in Heads by Dennis in town. I think she's in love with Dennis.

HER CELTIC TWIN: Deirdre, very beautiful and the cause of Ulster's sorrows. Once she married Conchobhar, she remained sad and eventually threw herself from his speeding chariot and smashed her brains out on a rock.

MY TWIN: Dexter. By now you've noticed that he's the only one in the family whose name doesn't begin with M? That's Dad's doing. Mom insisted all her children have names that begin with M. It helps the magic. But by the time Dexter and I came along, Dad said, "No more." So he claimed Dexter, who is very handsome and all the girls are nuts over him, but he's too modest to acknowledge it. He wears his hair short, with some kind of fancy cowlick. He's going out for football this fall. And here's the sad thing: Dex believes in magic. He knows a lot, too. Knows the toad is a water spirit, that poplar leaves tremble because Jesus was crucified on a cross of poplar. Knows the reason a horse breathes on water before drinking: because sometimes water sleeps, and to drink sleeping water is to die.

His problem is, he wants to be a normal kid but he also wants to have magic. I'd give him mine if I could.

His Celtic Twin? I couldn't find one for Dexter. Maybe his spirit still has to more fully evolve, I don't know.

I'm sure mine does, too. There's so much I don't know, in spite of all the training Aunt Melanie has given me, that it scares me sometimes. And do you know what's even scarier? She says I'll find out all that I don't know, soon enough. In my own way and time.

"But only when you move into what you fear," she says. "Only when you face your life in its entirety and face up to your own behavior and decisions. And learn if your difficulties are the result of your own inner turmoil."

You see why I'm scared? Wouldn't you be?

Chapter
One

E ver since he came home to Glen Laurel to stay, my brother Mac wanted me to go to regular school.

But first he wanted Dex on the school bus.

Dex had never ridden the school bus and he was eight. He was afraid of it. He dreamed, he told Mom, that it went into the river and all the kids drowned. That was when he was just in kindergarten, but a five-year-old's dream was a prophecy to Mom, so she got both of us in the car every morning and drove Dex to school.

Dad was still home then, and a couple of times he tried to get Dex on the bus. But Dex would bawl like a stuck pig, so Dad let it be.

All through first and second grade, Mom drove Dex to school. Things must have been building up in Dad about then, because he left shortly afterward and Mac came home and said, What the hell is this, and came every morning for a week and stood in front of the house next to Dex and then picked him up and put him on the bus.

Dex cried his heart out for the first week in that bus. And Mom cried hers out inside the house. And after the bus pulled away, Mac would turn and look at me, sitting there on the front step, watching, and I'd run into the house. Because I knew he wanted me on that bus, too. I knew he was pushing for it. But Mom and the aunts charmed him, so he gave in.

After the first week, you couldn't keep Dex off the bus. He loved it. And it didn't go into the river. But then, last year, on a cold, rainy, windy morning in December, on the way to school, Dex's dream came true.

An electric wire came loose and hit the school bus on its right rearview mirror. The driver, Mrs. Wilson, called for help, but her phone didn't work. Already, the bus's tires were smoking, so Mrs. Wilson got all the kids out the emergency back door. She was very brave, because no sooner were they all out than the bus burst into flames.

Of course, Mac came with the fire and police people. And Mrs. Wilson told him Dex had helped the little kids out first and was the last one off.

Mac was both scared for Dex and proud of him. I think Dex felt the same way about himself.

"Am I brave?" he asked me later, when we were discussing it.

"Yes, Dex. You're brave."

"I was scared, too. But Mac said that was okay. Tell me, Millicent, is a fire as good as the river for making a dream come true?"

"I think so. Aunt Melanie says water is life-giving and life-destroying. And that fire is a creator and a destroyer. So I think the fire made your dream come true."

"Does it mean I have magic?" he asked me.

I knew he wanted magic, bad. "I think you have some magic, Dex. Aunt Melanie says everybody in the family does."

"Even Mac?"

"Sure. But Aunt Melanie says he believes in his lights that flash on the car and in his radio that crackles, and that his gun is his magic wand and his badge is his pentacle."

"What's a pentacle?"

"It was the shield of the ancient hunter and warrior. Aunt Melanie says it's really a symbol of peace, that it acts like a magnet, drawing energy to it."

"Oh." He grinned. "You're learning so much cool stuff."

"Yeah."

"But I gotta tell you, Millicent. Mac's talking about you going to regular school soon. I heard him tell Mom he's not gonna put up with this much longer. Eighth grade, he says. Next year."

Aunt Melanie had said we couldn't hold Mac off much longer. Now she begged him, "Darling, don't take her away from us yet." And Aunt Mercy said that she was going to have me volunteer at the hospital as part of my eighth-grade studies.

What could Mac do? Three grown women who knew magic fluttering around him and calling him darling. They got eighth grade out of him.

Then he put his foot down. "No more. She starts high school in the fall," I heard him say one night. The aunts and Mac had come for supper, which was over. They were having an after-dinner drink in the great room. Dex and I were sent up to do our homework. I wasn't supposed to be listening.

"I love you all, but it's enough," Mac said.

"She's just coming into her Power," Aunt Melanie argued.

"That's why it's enough," Mac answered. "She's not running around with grapes in her hair anymore, or mouthing off about suppressed desires."

"Darling, you aren't going to forbid her from practicing her magic?" Mom asked.

I was up on the landing. I heard the silence that followed. Then Mac's gruff voice. "I want her to be a normal human being."

"Does that mean no magic?" Mom pushed. "Think of what she could accomplish!"

Mac answered, slowly and gently, "Mom, don't you know that a normal life, with all the boring, everyday ins and outs, spouse, kids, a dog and cat, all the ups and downs, is the biggest accomplishment of all? Do you know how few people really get that? How precious it is?"

"I'd say it was cruel of you to say that to me, if you hadn't lost it, too," Mom answered. "But still. You're going to forbid her magic? Like your father forbade mine?"

What did *that* mean?

"Let's put it this way," Mac said. "I'm going to use all the influence I have to make her a normal, responsible, contributing human being. And I'll thank you all not to use any spells, curses, or magic potions to stop me."

"We don't use spells," Aunt Mercy said. "Not bad ones, anyway."

"I don't want you to use even good ones," Mac insisted. "I can't work against that stuff. You've got to promise."

"You act as if you have to save her from us," Aunt Melanie accused.

"I'm sorry. I don't mean to. You've all done a good job of nurturing and loving her. You've done the woman thing, and I'm grateful. But just don't stop me from doing what I have to do. And don't warn her off me. We'll all do what we consider best for her, and may the best man win. Okay?"

"He's thrown down the gauntlet," Aunt Mercy said.

"And she adores him," from Aunt Melanie.

"He's going to try to convince her to reject her Power," from Aunt Mercy.

"Is that what you're going to do, darling?" Mom asked.

Mac didn't say he was and he didn't say he wasn't. "Do you all promise?" he pushed.

They promised. No spells, no stacking the deck against him. They wouldn't even warn me.

"You've got Dexter," Aunt Melanie almost whined.

"I don't *have* Dexter. I don't want to have anybody. I just want to do my job with them. I'm taking her to register tomorrow. I'll need her birth certificate, Mom. And medical and academic records. I'll need them tonight. And have her dressed like a proper little girl. No ritual robes, angel wings, or moonstones in her hair. Please."

"She's not a little girl anymore," Aunt Melanie said.

"Well, she is to me," Mac returned. He was very polite about it. But then, Mac always was.

Mom must have kissed him then. "All right, Mac," I heard her say. "You've got her. But put down the whip and chair."

Next morning, Mom had me up and ready. I wore a gauzy pleated summer skirt and a short-sleeve ribbed top. Everything pale yellow. White sandals. Mom even pulled my hair back off my face and tied it with a slim black ribbon. Mac said nothing to me in the car, before or after I got registered for school, about last evening's conversation.

I made like I didn't know, of course. And I got myself ready for when he came at me about rejecting my Power. But he didn't. Not that morning, anyway.

What he did talk about was school. "When you go here, there's to be no talk about magic," he said. "Far as anybody is concerned, you're just a regular kid. Okay?"

I said okay. Then I said: "But they all know about us already. So what if they ask?"

"Tell them you can't talk about it. It isn't a lie. Remember, I was taught by Aunt Melanie, too. And I know what she says. That if you talk about it, it lessens the Power. I want you to concentrate on social skills and your studies."

"But I'm not a regular kid."

"I'm not kidding about this, Millicent. Don't crowd me."

He was acting different, not like the Mac who'd seen Dex and me through the last five years, sometimes with a tenderness nobody would believe.

In the principal's office, he acted proud of me. "My little sister, Dave. You know her. Home-schooled till now, but she's smart as hell. Good kid, too."

They'd gone to high school together, before I was born.

I wanted to just bust when he said that stuff about me. And when he pulled out the documents, Mr. Rudolphi, the principal, looked up in surprise. "I didn't know you were legally responsible for your brother and sister," he said.

That's how modest Mac was about it. And private. Not everybody knew it. After all, we lived with Mom. Right then, he all but puffed up trying to be modest about it. "Yeah, the ball's in my court, Dave," he said.

Then he sent me out of the office. Outside in the hall, though, I heard what he said. "Let me know if they give you any problems, Dave. No special treatment. I'll handle it."

Afterward, in the car, he still held the whip and chair, as Mom described it.

"I'm not fooling," he said. "With the magic stuff. It's the way it has to be."

That afternoon, Naomi Carlson came knocking on my front door for the first time. "Heard you're gonna start high school in the fall," she said.

Her sandy hair fell straight and stringy to her shoulders. Her eyes couldn't decide whether to be blue or gray, because, as I was soon to learn, they were too busy deciding who could be conned and who couldn't. She was full in the bust already. She had an ankle tattoo and silver earrings with the feminist movement symbol dripping from her ears. She wore lip gloss and purple toenail polish and exposed her midriff.

Most of the time she ran around in her mother's old, tattered wedding dress.

I had no real friends outside the family. I spent my leisure time shooting baskets with Dex, reading, making Babylonian devil traps, or learning about herbs and magic.

I invited her in. "Wow," she said, looking around the great room. "Some digs. Heard your father built this place before he ran off. Will you show me around?"

So I did. And I told her about the old ironmonger who lived in the house during the Revolutionary War. "He fixed muskets for the Americans. Then he turned his coat and started giving those muskets to the British. He was hanged under a full moon right outside. And on stormy nights you can still hear him banging away in the cellar."

"Wow!"

"And in the Civil War, a man lived here who made shoes for the army. But they were so cheap, they fell apart. A barefooted, wounded soldier came to the front door one day and shot him right on the doorstep."

"What's that for?" She pointed to the raised platform of polished wood in the middle of the great room. It was the size of a boxing ring and had a wooden carved railing all around it. On chains from the cathedral ceiling on two sides hung stained-glass medieval scenes.

"My dad did that. He used to sit there with me and Dexter when we were crawling around, and read his newspaper."

"Awesome."

I shrugged. "Someday, maybe I'll show you my aunts' bed-and-breakfast. Al Capone once hid out in this town, you know. He stayed in that house. They have an Al Capone room."

We went up the stairway that had a landing big enough so that Mom had a chair, table, and lamp on it. "You can look right down on the whole great room from here," Naomi said.

"The end where you come in the front door is what my dad called the library." Bookcases lined the wall at that end.

"Is it true that the town was overrun with stills during Prohibition?" she asked.

I said yes.

"And that during World War Two they ran black market goods out of Glen Laurel, too?"

I said yes. In my room, she bounced on my bed, admired my dream catcher, my medium-sized black cauldron, and my green leather book embossed in gold. "What is that?" she asked.

"My Book of Shadows."

Her eyes widened. "What does that mean?"

"My personal journal. In it, I'm supposed to put my magical adventures. The only reason it's called that is because in medieval times you had to keep your practices to yourself. So people wrote in it under shadow of night. Or you could be burned at the stake for being a witch, especially if you were a woman."

"Are you people witches?"

"No. Nothing of the sort. We just have magic. Do you know why they started putting witches to death in 1022?"

"No, tell me."

"Well, first off, it was women they wanted to put to death. Our early ancestors worshiped the great goddesses. Then men took over and made the warrior-hunter cult. They feared women because they controlled life. That was their way of getting rid of some of them."

"Wow. So that's what your aunt is teaching you. Can I light a cigarette?"

"No," I said. "Mom might smell the smoke."

If it hadn't been for her coming from the wrong side of town, her father being in prison, her older sister dancing in the topless bar out on the highway, I would have thought somehow that Mac had sent her around to help me be normal. Because the first thing she did, after bouncing on my bed, was say, "You poor kid. Up until now I've been on the bottom of the food chain with the girls in school. I just wanted to meet my replacement. Hey, you want me to clue you in? Somebody has to."

She clued me in about everybody in school, who was vicious and who was just plain snotty, who had the best clothes, who lied, who cheated on tests, who you didn't talk to in the girls' room, who thought they were God's gift, and who were the nerds.

She told me who took drugs, who didn't, how to stay away from the cheerleaders, and what boys not to talk to because "they only want one thing."

She gave me a crash course in survival. Then her eyes lighted on the framed picture of my sister Martha. "She the one who they say died?"

"She did die," I said.

She didn't say any more. I thought her way of putting it was peculiar. Did she know something about Martha, like she knew about the kids in school? Next she saw my dad's picture.

"He's sexy," she said.

He was wearing a hard hat, his face was tan, and he was grinning. "I suppose he's handsome," I said.

"You suppose? And what about that brother of yours? He's a hunk. Too bad he's a cop. Oh, there's one more thing I should tell you about school. If any of them come up to you and want to be friends, you'll have to be careful."

"Why?"

"Because they'll want you to work some magic, that's why."

I hadn't thought about that. I thanked her again.

"It would be nice now if you shared something with me."

I showed her my electronic black box that Aunt Melanie had given me last Christmas. "It's a spontaneous psychophysical incident data electronic recorder," I explained. "SPIDER for short. It can record ghost sightings."

"You ever use it?"

"I've tried, in our basement when I hear the old ironmonger banging away. Trouble is, most ghosts appear for five to thirty seconds only. The box comes from Great Britain."

"Wanna share secrets?"

I knew I wasn't good at this girlie stuff, but I wanted to be. "Sure."

"Okay. My dad's getting out of prison soon. Only you can't

tell anybody. 'Specially not that hotshot cop brother of yours."

"Okay."

"I've visited my dad. You ever visit anybody in prison?"

"No."

"It's neat. You get to watch all the wives and husbands trying to hold and kiss. Now you tell me something."

I wanted to impress her, to hold on to her as a friend. "I can't lie," I said. "Or I'll lose my Power."

Her eyes widened. "Never?"

"Never."

"What a bummer."

"Yeah."

I could tell she was impressed. She asked me a lot about my magic then, my Power. I told her some things, then acted mysterious. "If you talk about it too much, it lessens it," I said.

She respected that. She was awed by the whole thing. And I really expected her to ask me to do some magic for her. I couldn't. I wasn't ready yet. But she didn't ask. When she left, she said, "Wanna be friends?" And I said "Sure." And she and I were friends that whole unbelievable summer. And into the fall, which was even more unbelievable.

Chapter
Two

"You should get a tattoo on your ankle," Naomi said. "A rose. Or maybe one of your magic symbols."

"I would love it," I said. "But I know better than to ask Mac. And even my aunts wouldn't permit it."

"You're too dependent on your family. You have to start breaking away. I thought all your magic was supposed to do that for you."

We were at her house watching soap operas, a week after we'd met. Her mother was at work. She was a hairdresser, like my sister, at Heads by Dennis. We had to be quiet because her sister, Darla, who worked nights as a dancer, was sleeping.

We each had a pencil and pad and kept score of all the vases of flowers in the scenes. We laughed at them. "What house has vases of fresh flowers like that in every room?" Naomi asked.

It was only one of the things she pointed out to me. She considered it her personal duty, she said, to raise my consciousness.

And the more I got to know her, the more I envied her. Not only that she had the guts to run around in her mother's old wedding gown, which made her daring and inventive. Not only that her imagination worked six ways at once. But because she had total freedom. She did pretty much as she pleased. No mom or aunts hovering. No brother to answer to.

I wanted to be part of that freedom. Oh, I wanted it so bad!

"Get the tattoo anyway," she said. "What can they do, once you've done it? You can say you're my cousin. Darla will take us and vouch for you."

"I'd have a shelf life as short as organic bread when Mac saw it."

"What would he do? Does he hit you?"

"No."

"So, then?"

I thought of Mac, the way the hands would be on the hips, the breath would be let out slowly, trying for patience, the look of disappointment that would be in the eyes. "It's just that we have this thing. It'd be turning on him. I couldn't do it."

"Boy, he's got you on a short leash, doesn't he? You've got to assert yourself with him sometime. This would be making a statement. Like I do when I wear my mother's wedding gown."

"What have you got to make a statement about?"

"I'm showing what I think of my parents' marriage. Haven't you noticed how ragged the gown is? Anyway, people can interpret my wearing it the way they want. If they can't handle it, it's their problem, not mine. Wanna go to the church and paint the Virgin Mary's toenails purple? Nobody'll be there this time of day."

She'd talked of doing this before, so I wasn't shocked. I

25

felt I had to say yes. After all, I couldn't be chicken about everything.

We painted the Virgin Mary's toenails purple. Her feet were bare, since she was standing on a serpent. I told Naomi that we should be doing pale pink. "Purple is aligned with chaos," I said.

"Welcome, chaos."

We were Catholic in our family. And this was our church, St. Sebastian's. My sister Martha was buried in the churchyard. Aunt Melanie said I had all the Catholic conscience and Catholic guilt. Aunt Melanie also said that after men took over the world with the warrior-hunter cult, the Church realized we needed a nurturing source. So they gave us the Virgin Mary.

We must be breaking some commandment, I decided. So I knew this was wrong, and felt we were committing blasphemy somehow. I couldn't wait to get out of there.

The next morning was Saturday, and when the phone rang early and Mom called upstairs to say Mac was coming over to take me to breakfast, I sensed doom.

We'd been found out! But would he be taking me to breakfast, then? What was going on? My hands shook as I dressed. It was a bright summer morning. But I went downstairs feeling like I was being summoned to the Inquisition.

Apparently, it wasn't the Virgin Mary's toenails that he had on his mind, though it was clear that something serious was bothering him.

He kissed me lightly on the cheek. Then Mom said: "Be a good girl, now. Remember, your brother loves you."

What was this? An early morning sacrifice to the gods of

fertility? He didn't talk much in the car. Then we went by St. Sebastian's. A police car was out front. The cop was talking to one of the priests. Mac tooted the horn and waved.

"What do you know about that?" he said. "Some damn kids vandalized the Virgin Mary. Painted her toenails. Do you believe it?"

I said nothing. The word "vandalized" sounded so awful. And I felt so guilty. There was a firm rule in our family. Dex and I were never to do anything to embarrass Mac in his position as police chief. Or mar our name in the community.

"I'd give a good scare to those kids who did it."

Mac didn't go to church anymore, since his divorce. But he made me and Dex go with Mom on Sundays. Now I wanted to confess to him, tell him I was one of those kids. And I was scared already. But I didn't.

He took me to the diner out on the highway. The food was good, homestyle, and lots of cops went there. I waited to see what was coming. It came with the ham and eggs.

"I guess you know something's up, huh?"

I nodded yes.

He sipped his coffee and leaned back in the booth. "Okay, you know I don't beat around the bush. I want you to think, seriously, about rejecting your Power when the time comes, Millicent."

His blue eyes were kind, his voice tender. He reached across the table and put his large hand over mine. His was warm, reassuring. Mine, cold as ice.

"You all right?" he asked. "You're shaking."

"Uh-huh."

"Were you expecting this?"

I shrugged.

"Look, I have to do this. It's part of my responsibility. If Dexter had the Power, I'd confront him, too, but he doesn't. I have my reasons, and they're good ones. I want you to just listen, okay?"

I said I'd listen.

"Eat," he gestured with his fork. "Go ahead, you look like you need it."

I ate. But I didn't need food. I needed some of Naomi's daring. But I had none of it, not an ounce. He ate, too.

"You know I love you," he said. "So I wouldn't do anything to hurt you or cheat you out of anything that's right for you. Do you trust me on that?"

"Yes, Mac." I did. Damn it, I did. In spite of Naomi and my aunts, in spite of the thrill of my magic, I did. I got a sharp pain in my head. Two sharp pains. Swords clashing, I thought. There was no doubt about it.

"First, I want you to have a good life," he was saying. "That doesn't mean being rich, or even being a big success. Most people today have got it all wrong. It means home and family, a decent guy for a husband, some cute kids, being part of a community. All kinds of people think it's their right and their due, Millicent, but most mess up at it. I did."

"No, Mac," I objected.

He held up his fork to silence me.

"Your sister did. Our aunts did. Mom did, no matter how much we love her. I have to tell you that. And do you know why?"

I didn't answer. Did he expect me to?

"Because of the magic in our family. The Power. It messes everybody up. It messed up Mom's marriage, Maddie's life, and more than I can tell you about right now."

"What more?"

"It's Mom's place to tell you. And she will, soon. I've asked her."

What? What was he talking about? Something. Something bad hovering over his head. I knew about auras, how to read them, and his was fractured.

"And when Mom tells you, you'll understand what I mean, about how magic ruined our family. And I want you to give a lot of thought to what she says. I don't want to force my will on you, but you have to be informed. Besides," he grinned at me, that lopsided grin of his with all the great white teeth that somehow broke my heart. "Besides, you don't need magic or special powers, honey. You've got everything going for you. More than most girls. Looks. Yeah, I know I never say, but you've got great skin and bones and hair and, well, soon you'll have a great figure. You're on your way to being a knockout. And you've got good genes and brains. Besides which, you'll never be one of those bitchy women people hate so much. I promise you that."

I glowed under the praise, even while I hated myself for needing it.

"So what do you need magic for, huh? You tell me." He leaned across the table and took my hand again. "I promise you, Millicent, it'll bring trouble. It always does. So think, seriously, about rejecting it. Okay?"

I said I would. We finished our meal talking about other things. When we left the diner, his arm was around my shoulder. Then he opened the car door and hugged me. "I expect you to do the right thing about this," he said.

I got into the police car, put on my seat belt, and watched him get in and buckle his. He was wearing regular clothes, pullover knit shirt and slacks, summer jacket. I knew that under the jacket he was wearing his gun, which Aunt called his magic wand, and his badge, which was a shield that drew energy to it like a magnet.

The police radio crackled.

Damn love, I thought, that's the thing I've got to worry about, that's the Power I've got to reject. That's what he's using on me. Unfair! I felt worse than I had in a long time.

Mac had taught Dex and me to shoot baskets, to play chess, to work on our computers, to fish and swim and ride our two-wheelers. He represented everything that was sane and safe, straight and aboveboard in the world. And now he wanted me to be that way, too.

I went home and up to my room and cried. And then Mom came up and sat on the bed and put her hand on my shoulder. "I know," she said. "Cry if you must. That's part of it all. The Power has its price, Millicent. It isn't free."

I rolled onto my back to look at her. "Mac says you've got something to tell me," I said.

Mom lay down on the bed next to me. We both lay, without touching, looking up at the ceiling.

"In the beginning, when your dad and I were planning marriage," she said, "he asked me to give up my magic, too. He said I was beautiful and smart, and our love was all the magic we needed."

"He sounds like Mac."

"Mac takes after his father in many ways."

"So you never used your Power?"

"No."

"Why didn't you use it before you met him?"

"Because I was foolish. I was always saying no, tomorrow there will be a better reason. And then I met your father. And I gave up my Power. Oh, I still practiced my magic, though he didn't like it. I could never completely give it up. And that's what I have to tell you."

"What, Mom?"

"It ruined my marriage anyway in the end. Even without the Power. And it ruined a lot of things for a lot of people."

"How?"

She sighed. I leaned closer to her and felt the sigh become a tremor in her body. I held her.

"Your sister Martha. It was my fault she died."

The tremor transferred to my body. "But she died of complications from chicken pox."

"That's what we told you and Dexter."

"Mom . . ."

"Hush, let me tell it. This isn't easy for me. But I promised your brother I would tell it. I was expecting you and Dexter when she died. Martha was seven, Madeleine was ten, and Mac was going on eighteen. I was out walking in the woods with Martha one day. I came upon this enormous tree, near the river, where the half-finished house is. So beautiful it was. Trees are magic, you know."

"I know. Is that the one whose heartbeat I listen to by the house?"

"Yes. Anyway, I was feeling down, and this tree was emitting such soothing energies. It had such a oneness with life, and I sensed its wonderful soul. I knew that if I could get a piece of the bark and wear it for the rest of my pregnancy, I would have an easy delivery. I got so absorbed in getting the bark, I forgot about Martha."

31

What was she telling me? I couldn't absorb the thought.

"I was concentrating so hard. I'd put myself sort of into a trance, I guess. I never even heard the splash. And when I went looking for her, she had drowned!"

I felt my body stiffen. I pulled away from her. I looked at her, lying there on the bed next to me. My mom was in her early fifties, still beautiful, with gray-green eyes. She wears her tawny, gray-streaked hair straight. Not many women can do this, but the hair adds to her attractiveness. She has crinkles around her eyes, a round face, and the sweetest smile.

I couldn't stop staring at her, the mom I knew. "She drowned?" Why had nobody ever told me this?

I sat up, gulping for air. Thoughts whirled in my head like the overhead ceiling fan, round and round, going nowhere.

But making sense. That was the worst part of it.

"She drowned," I said again. "That's what you're saying, Mom? By the tree I love so much? And the bend in the river where the house is? My secret place?"

She put one hand on her forehead, then over her eyes, as if to block out some vision. "I hailed a car from the road. The man got out, and we took her to the hospital. But it was too late."

"She drowned?" It was all I could think of to say. My head was pounding. I couldn't believe this! They'd lied to me, all of them! To me and Dexter! "Mom," I said. "Oh, Mom!"

I got off the bed. I walked around it. I looked at the picture of a smiling Martha on my bookcase. Drowned? With Mom right there? I walked around to the other side of the bed and looked down at her. Her eyes were closed. Tears were coming down her face. I took her hand. It was ice cold.

"Mom?" I said. "Mom?"

She withdrew her hand. "I'm all right, darling. As all right as I ever have been since then." She sat up on the edge of the bed and pushed her hair back. Then she reached for my hand and forced a smile. "It's the real reason your daddy left. Not because of the money he lost on that house. Oh, he didn't leave right then. Bless him, he stayed. For eight more years. But it wasn't any good. Everything was broken between us. We tried to comfort each other, but it didn't work. I blamed him and he blamed me."

"Why did you blame him, Mom?"

"Because he made me reject my Power. If I'd had it, I could have saved Martha."

"But maybe you would have used it already."

"I don't think so. I was always saving it. Anyway, that's all I ever thought about. And of course, he blamed me because it was my fault. He tried not to, but I know he did!"

"Wow, Mom!" Tears came to my eyes. "That's so heavy for you."

She got up and put her arm around me. "Yes. Very heavy. And it affected Mac because after that happened, he rejected all magic. And Maddie saw our marriage disintegrating, and got more confused than ever."

"And that's why Daddy left Mac in charge of me and Dexter?"

"Yes. He didn't trust me. I don't blame him."

"Well, he could have taken us with him." Too late, then, I realized what I'd said. "I didn't mean that, Mom. I wouldn't want to be away from you. But Maddie's no prize. And Mac drives me crazy. You don't know what he did to me this morning."

She hugged me. "Oh, darling, but I do know. Because

your father did it to me. Only Mac has his reasons. He's doing the job I could never do. He just wants you to be a responsible and happy human being. Not like me. I'm a failure."

"Don't say that, Mom. Nobody's better than you. You've been a great mother to me and Dexter. Accidents happen. Don't make something mystical out of it."

"It's the reason I agreed not to let Dexter have the Power. I tried to make things up to your father. So you see, everybody was affected."

"Why didn't Mac save Martha? He was eighteen."

"He was still apprenticing. But he fooled around a lot. Football came first. Aunt Melanie often scolded him for it. He blames himself for that. Then after Martha died, he rejected it anyway."

"Mom, you know, I feel a special pull to that place where Martha drowned. Why?"

"Her spirit is probably there. Open your psyche to it. Don't be afraid."

"What am I going to do about my Power, Mom?"

She pulled away, hands on my shoulders, and looked down at me. "My darling girl. You do what you think is best. Whatever you do, I'll love you and back you up. But I'll never try to influence you. All right?"

I groaned. That was no help. "Sure, Mom," I said.

Chapter Three

"I hope you were sympathetic to your mother when she told you," Aunt Melanie said. "And supportive."

"And not too shocked," Aunt Mercy added.

It was the next day, Sunday. Of course they'd heard about my breakfast with Mac, and how Mom had finally told me about Martha. I was helping them get the tea things in the front parlor. All the weekend guests were gone.

They had decided it was time for a meeting, and Mom was on her way.

"I was shocked," I admitted. "But I was supportive."

Mom came and we had an old-fashioned tea party, only instead of cakes, my aunts had made sourdough bread in the shape of a Celtic knot. Aunt Melanie poured tea out of her ancient silver pot that came from Lady Sybil. "The one answer Mercy and I can give you is that only you can decide about your Power. If you really want to reject it, then it won't work for you. But if you're doing it only to please your brother, you'll still have it."

"Mom rejected hers and really didn't want to," I argued.

"I wanted to," Mom said. "For your dad. I loved him so."

"What do *you* want?" Aunt Mercy asked. "Remember that you must have the level of energy for magic. That you must truly desire it, and be totally, even lustfully involved. And if your enthusiasm is not there, it will not work."

I looked at the three women who had taught me everything I knew about my Power and magic over the years. Tears came to my eyes. I don't know what I would have done without my aunts. They were so important in my life. I feel sorry for people who don't have aunts. They tell us family secrets. They knew our mothers as girls. They see us more as people than our parents do. They can be friends, even a bit naughty at times. It's fun to do things with them. I think aunts are very important in a person's spiritual development.

And of course, it went without saying what I felt for Mom.

"I want to keep it," I said. "But I don't want to hurt Mac."

"Then in heaven's name," Aunt Melanie said, reaching for a bottle of dandelion wine and putting a teaspoonful in her tea, "keep it. You are certainly educated enough in creative visualization, concentration, focusing your personal energy sources, and manifesting your highest ideals, not to be put off by Mac's foibles."

"You can still love and respect him, and obey him in all earthly matters," Aunt Mercy added. "But this magic is a wonderful tool that can enhance your life if used properly. And the time is coming soon for you to pass your test, so you will qualify for it."

"What have you decided to do for your test?" Aunt Melanie asked.

I smiled. "Shape-shifting."

"Quite a test." Aunt Mercy now reached for the dandelion wine. I knew that it increased clairvoyance for divination, but

I wasn't allowed to have any yet. "I can see there's no shilly-shallying with you, sweetie. Well, you must drink plenty of pennyroyal tea to strengthen your resolve."

Mom reached for the dandelion wine. "Is there any reason," she asked, "why Mac has to know what she has determined to do?" She looked at me. "Did he give you a time frame for an answer, Millicent?"

"No."

Aunt Melanie lighted a cigarette. Her eyes narrowed. "Do you think, Mercy, that Mac remembers the exact date when her Power will be given?"

"I don't think so," Aunt Mercy said. "I think he just knows it's to come soon."

"Then is there any reason we have to tell him?" Mom asked.

We looked at each other. "Only if he asks," Aunt Melanie said. "Remember, she can't lie. I think if he doesn't ask, you shouldn't volunteer the information, Millicent. Do you think you can carry this off, until you do your test and receive your Power?"

Aunt Mercy shook her head. "She can never keep a secret from Mac," she said.

"I can," I told them. "And I have." And then I told them about the Virgin Mary's purple toenails.

Their eyes widened. Then they burst into laughter. The more they envisioned it, the more their laughter increased. I think the dandelion wine helped. Soon they couldn't stop, even Mom. Tears were coming down Aunt Melanie's face. "Oh, God forgive us," she said. "Your brother is the most decent, darling man. And we're not encouraging you to dis-obey him, Millicent, and I promise you that if you start doing so, I will personally spank you. But painting the Virgin's toenails!"

Another round of laughter.

"She can keep a secret from Mac, all right," Aunt Mercy said. "All right, all right, everything's going to be all right, Millicent. You keep your own good counsel. Love your brother, obey him, but every time you find yourself wanting to talk about some magic to him, think of the Virgin Mary's toenails."

All that summer I hung out with Naomi. We went to the movies. We went to the Dolphin Swim Club, where Mom had a family membership. On afternoons after Darla woke up and went out, Naomi and I went through her costumes in her bedroom and tried them on. Naomi showed me how to put on false eyelashes and make up my face as if I were on stage.

One night, in the middle of the week, Aunt Melanie let me invite Naomi to the bed-and-breakfast, and we slept in the Al Capone room. We walked on the very floorboards where he walked.

"I wonder what woman he had in here with him," Naomi said.

We read *Playboy* magazine. I'd never seen it. I think Dex had a copy in his room, but he never let me see it. My eyes bulged. "Those women are violating their own Power," I said. "They will never be identical with the energies of life."

Naomi stared at me like I was crazy. "Call it what you want. They're making plenty of money."

"After posing like that, they'll never be able to commit to a relationship with another human being."

Naomi laughed. "You sound like a little parrot."

"Women's bodies are sacred. They're all tied in with fertility and birth."

"Who told you that garbage? Mac?"

"No. My aunts. Let's do something else."

It was a hot day. We got on our bikes and rode to a produce stand where they had a petting farm for kids—goats, chickens, pigs, and rabbits.

"You look at those bunny rabbits there in the heat in those cages," Naomi said. "Look how they're panting. Want to let them loose?"

She was right. They were suffering. There was only one lady under the awning, serving customers. We wandered through the petting farm, and, one by one, without anybody realizing it, we opened the latches of the cages and let the bunnies loose.

Then we got on our bikes and left.

Naomi was right that time. I felt good doing it. I didn't feel a bit of guilt about it at all.

On the Fourth of July a terrible thing happened in Glen Laurel. And it happened in Naomi's part of town.

She lived where the original town had been, in the bottomland by the river. But the river flooded once too often for people there to get help from the government anymore, so years ago they moved the town farther up the hill.

Some people just stayed, including Naomi's family. And every three years or so they got flooded out again, and you'd see their sad piles of belongings stacked up outside the houses while everybody cleaned up inside.

There are abandoned buildings where stores used to be. I think the only outsiders who go there are Jehovah's

Witnesses, and kids from the new part of town who are looking for trouble.

On the Fourth of July, JoLynn Eustis, who was fifteen,
tumbled off the roof of one of those old houses, where she'd
been watching the fireworks with Lisle Hansen, and was
killed.

The coroner determined she'd been taking drugs.
Ecstasy.

Mac nearly went into spontaneous combustion. A little
girl dead! For no reason! He ranted and raved for days.
He lectured Dex and me, though we hadn't done anything.
He had a meeting with Mr. Rudolphi at the high school and
made arrangements for his people to take part in the D.A.R.E.
program and go into the schools and talk about drugs. He got
depressed.

"He blames himself," Mom said.

"Why?" Dex and I asked.

But Mom didn't answer.

Aunt Melanie brought carnations into his house to ward
off negativity, and a white heather plant to attract positive
energy. She even put rosemary under his pillow for peaceful
sleep.

Mac eventually snapped out of it, by throwing himself
into the D.A.R.E. program and forbidding me to go to that
part of town again.

"But my friend lives there!" I argued.

"Have her come here. I mean it, Millicent. Try me if you
don't think I mean it."

Naomi took it pretty well, considering. For the rest of the
summer she came to my house. August flew like a sparrow

fleeing from a blue jay.

School would be starting soon. It was the twenty-fourth of August. Dex was going out for football and went to practice every day.

Mom did a spell for his protection and made him special foods. Aunt Melanie made him drink horehound tea for protection and healing. Mac gave him his old jersey to practice in.

Summer was finished, used up, tired. I sensed, somehow, that once school started I would lose Naomi as a friend. I didn't want that. I liked her, in spite of all her weirdness, her crudeness, and her occasional unkindnesses. I liked her because she was outside of my family. Different. Separate. And when I was with her, I felt different and separate, too.

"Fat chance," she said when I told her. "Only way that'd happen is if you desert me. I told you, I'm the lowest there is on the food chain."

Still, I wanted to make up for not being allowed to come to her house. "I'd like us to make a blood promise to be friends," I told her.

"Is this a magic thing?"

"No. Just a friend thing. But you can't break it or bad luck might come. It has to do with trusting each other. Want to do it?"

"Sure. Where?"

I'd given it thought. "At my secret place. Tomorrow afternoon. I'll bring the stuff. And some Coke and potato chips."

"We'll spend the afternoon," she said. "I'll bring nail polish. We can do our toenails. You want pink or purple?"

"Pink."

"If purple is good enough for the Virgin Mary, it's good enough for me," she said.

* * *

Naomi looked around. "Where are the Indian graves?"

I hadn't been there since Mom told me that this was the very spot where Martha had drowned. The bend in the river, where the stone ledge went out. Likely she'd fallen from it. How would I feel about this place now? Was Martha's spirit there?

"Over there." I pointed.

"Let's walk on them."

"No." I grabbed the satin sleeve of her mother's wedding gown.

She looked at my hand. "Take your arm off the satin," she directed.

I did. "It isn't right to walk on anybody's grave. I respect your mother's wedding gown. You should respect this burial ground."

She shrugged and sat down. "Keep your old Indians. Let's paint our toenails.

"When you get married, who's going to give you away?" she asked. "Your father? Or Mac?"

I thought it was a trick question. She was full of them.

"I don't know," I said.

"You'll be in a fix then, let me tell you."

What was I supposed to say? I said nothing.

"I miss you coming to my house. Doesn't that brother of yours know people get killed everywhere?"

"Yes. But I have to humor him in this, Mom says."

"Does he think people in your neighborhood aren't on drugs?"

"He knows better. He's made a blood vow to get rid of drugs in Glen Laurel."

She took out a cigarette and lighted it. The action seemed so natural to her. I felt a surge of envy.

"You're so faithful to that family of yours. They don't tell you the truth about everything, you know."

I looked up. "Like what?"

She shrugged. "My mom's been in this town a long time. And being a hairdresser, she gets to hear everything."

"So does my sister Maddie."

"My mom's been here longer. And she says your sister Martha isn't buried in that churchyard. The stone they have there is just for appearances."

I felt a wave of shock. "Where is she buried, then?"

"She isn't."

"What?"

"She was cremated, my mom says. Your dad did it, because he knew he couldn't keep your mom from running to that churchyard. Her ashes are in a vase someplace. Probably in your mom's room."

I thought, with a dizziness in my head, about Mom's room. Were there any vases? I remembered one on the mantelpiece.

"Can you imagine being cremated?" she asked. "They burn your body!"

"Stop it, Naomi. You're so full of it. You make things up as you go along."

She shrugged. "Okay. Don't believe me. Just check all the vases in your mom's room, though."

We continued painting our toenails in silence for a moment. Then we let them dry and ate potato chips and drank Coke.

"My dad used to hit me and my sister with his belt when

he was home," she said.

Another bomb dropped on my psyche. I blinked. "I'm sorry, Naomi," I said.

"Did you ever get hit?"

"Maddie hit me a while back with a wooden spoon, because I sassed her. Mac stopped her and gave her hell."

She tossed her cigarette away. "Did you know your brother Mac is seeing my sister Darla?"

"Mac isn't seeing anybody. He likes Carol Mitchell, my piano teacher."

"He may like her, but he was out with Darla the other night. Came to pick her up."

My face flushed. I'd been hoping against hope for Carol and Mac to get back together. They belonged together! Carol was blond, plain, and sane as a preacher's wife. What would Mac do with Darla, a topless dancer? Not that she wasn't a nice person, and pretty, but still.

Mac? The most decent and darling man Aunt Melanie knew?

"I don't believe it," I said.

"Makes no never mind to me if you do or don't. But if they get hitched, that'll make us sisters. Sort of."

Mac and Darla? "He's been working with the township committee. They're getting up an ordinance to close down that place where Darla dances," I told her.

She grinned at me. "Well? See?"

I didn't. At least, I didn't want to. "Let's do our blood vow," I said. "It's getting late."

I wanted to do it before she changed her mind. It would really cement our friendship. I got out my stuff and we knelt on the floor in the half-finished house and each made a small cut in the other's palm, then clasped hands to make a blood promise of friendship.

"Friends forever," she said.

"No matter what," I returned.

Then we wrapped each other's hands with the gauze I'd brought. "My hand hurts," I said. "Does yours?"

"Sure, but I've got something to dull the pain." She took out a prescription vial from the drugstore. "Percocet. From Mom's medicine cabinet. It'll take away the pain. And it gives you a buzz. Want one?" She popped one in her mouth, took a swig of soda, and handed the vial to me.

Mac had told both Dex and me about drugs. Percocet was given to the football players when they had an injury. "Don't take any," he'd warned. Then he'd looked at me. "A lot of players give them to girls so they'll lose all their inhibitions and have sex."

"No, thanks," I said.

"Oh, Miss Goody Two-shoes. Big brother won't like it?"

"I don't need it," I snapped.

She flushed. "Sorry. Just remember our blood promise and what it means. It means no snitching. And breaking the promise is as good as lying."

"I know that, Naomi."

We stayed a little while longer. She asked me if I wanted to go to the mall that night with Darla and a friend. Darla would be driving.

"I have to ask Mom," I said. Then I gave her my orange triangle, my talisman. It has protective powers. I knew I could get another talisman from Aunt Melanie, and in spite of some of the mean things she'd said, I thought she needed it more than I did. And I still wanted her as a friend.

45

Chapter Four

A ctually, Mom had to clear it with Mac whenever Dex or I went "outside" town.

Our town is special. Some people think it's because of its history, or because artists, sculptors, and antique dealers have studios here. Or because there's so many new-money people building their McMansions in the wooded hills.

It's in the Northeast. I can't tell where. Mac would have to hire a dozen more police. We don't need any more tourists hanging around looking for a white doe at night that's really Aunt Melanie, or the tree with the heartbeat on the river bend. Or the miniature sunken city that's underwater there, where the maidens sing, who guide the river spirits at night. And where the undines, the water creatures, live.

You have to go over a wooden bridge to get here from the highway. There's no radio reception in cars for five miles out on the highway. When it floods, we're cut off from the rest of the world.

My people know it's an Otherworld where, if you believe, the leaves turn into diamonds at night, where the curtain between the visible and invisible worlds is like gauze, where druids live and sometimes are people you know.

It can be, according to your degree of belief, a place of wooded idylls, where pet dogs can suddenly become shining hounds, where a man can turn into Sir Lancelot, where magic cauldrons bubble in microwave ovens.

Aunt Melanie says there is a balance here, of good and evil, that only a few places in the world have.

She says that the few places in the world that have it determine if the world will give in to evil and chaos. And the people in this town help determine that every day.

For the most part, the townfolk stick pretty close. Mac enforces strict laws at the wishes of the Town Council. "We Take Care of Our Own," is the motto here. If someone is caught drunk, Mac wants his men to escort them home safely, unless they're harming someone. Houses have stickers in the windows that say "safe house," where kids can go if they are in trouble.

Mac started that. I think if he hadn't decided to come home on his own, the aunts would have done a spell and willed him home, to be here as police chief. They see him as the guardian of the whole town.

I think that's pretty scary. But then, that's my family.

Mac doesn't see any magic in Glen Laurel. He just doesn't want us running around far afield. But that day, Mom cleared it with him that I could go to the mall with Naomi. He said he'd be over after supper to give me money for sneakers for school.

I came downstairs, all ready to leave, and Mac was in the kitchen with Mom, having coffee. He lives in a bachelor pad in town, one of six condos Dad built along the river.

47

He gave me money. A hundred dollars. I'll say one thing for him, he isn't cheap. I know Daddy sends him money for me and Dex, and he has to account for every bit of it, but still.

I had on my old denim shorts that are kind of ragged at the edges and really short, and my favorite blue knit summer sweater. Blue awakens the emotions to the spiritual side of nature.

I was finally getting a respectable bust, and the sweater looked good on me. Then old Mac takes one look at me and says to Mom, "You're not gonna let her go out like that, are you?"

"Like what, darling?" Mom asks, like she hadn't told me earlier how nice my long legs looked, all browned from the sun. And how, since I lost seven pounds on Aunt Mercy's health diet, I looked better than ever.

Mac didn't answer. Just told me in a quiet voice to go upstairs and put on jeans or a skirt. "I'm not gonna have you running around the mall looking like that," he says.

I argued. "Everybody dresses like this."

"You're not everybody. How many times I gotta tell you that?"

"How would you like it if I ran around in Mom's old wedding gown, like Naomi does?" I shouldn't have said that. I knew, right off.

"Is she wearing it tonight?" Mac asked. "Because if she is, you're not going."

"Why does that child do that?" Mom asked.

"She says she's making a statement. The gown is ratty, she says, like her parents' marriage," I told Mom. Then I answered Mac. "Of course she isn't. But how would you like it if I did that?"

"It'd be the last statement you ever made," he shot back. Right from the hip. Acting tough. Oh, he was good at it, too.

It had been weeks since he'd asked me to give up my Power. He hadn't said another word about it, and neither had I. But there was something wrong between us now, negative forces at work.

He'd come down hard on me a few times in the last couple of weeks. And when Mac comes down hard on you, you sting, you hurt, even though he never raises a hand.

Tears come to your eyes. The world gets cold. And you hate him with a hate you never knew you had in you.

Mom gave me a look that meant, Go do as he says. So I did. I changed into jeans, then heard the car in the driveway.

I ran downstairs. Would Mac go outside when he saw Darla at the wheel? He did. But he was leaving, too. He went out with me, waved to Darla, and said hi. She waved back. Then he kissed me and got into his car.

If they were seeing each other, wouldn't there be more? But that's not the point. None of this is. The point is that I should have picked up on the symbolism there in the kitchen. All that business about legs. It was right in front of me and I didn't see it. I was just so mad at Mac that I didn't listen to my higher self.

The car came at us, right through the intersection outside the mall, and hit us in front, on the driver's side. I had my seat belt on, so did Naomi, and we were in back. All I did was hit my head inside the car. But it was hard enough so I was out of it for a while.

The noise was so loud you'd think seven dragons hit us. Then came the sound of shattering glass and screaming.

There was a lot of confusion. Darla was shrieking, "My leg, my leg, I can't feel my leg!"

Then there were police sirens, ambulances, and we were taken to the hospital.

I was scared. I started shaking and couldn't stop. I could hardly talk to the ambulance attendants, but they knew Mac and said he and Mom had been called. And sure enough, when we got to the hospital, Mom, Mac, and Dexter were there.

The doctor said the bump on my head wasn't serious but he would like to keep me overnight for observation. I wanted to go home, but Mac told me it was best to stay. "They have to make sure you don't have a concussion," he said.

I found out later that Darla's girlfriend had two broken ribs. Darla nearly had her leg cut off. You see what I mean about legs? And how the sign was right there in front of me earlier that night? But what was I supposed to do? Not go?

I was lying in bed in the hospital, feeling half out of it because of something they'd given me, feeling all kinds of guilt, because the others were so bad off and I figured Mom's protective magic had helped me.

Of course, Naomi was even luckier. They let her go home. Well, I'd given her my orange triangle, hadn't I?

Anyway, that's not the end of it. It was late, and Mom and Dex had left. A hospital room at night is a netherworld all on its own. Mac was half asleep in the chair. He'd been all undone, blaming himself. Mom had to tell him it wasn't his fault. And usually it's the other way around, with him reassuring her. We're great on guilt in this family, and guilt is a destructive force. We all know it but can't help it. I think it has to do with what happened to Martha.

That made me think of Dad. I dozed off thinking of him, then low voices startled me. Somebody switched a light on.

I opened my eyes, and then all of a sudden there he was.

My dad. Standing at the foot of my bed. At first I thought I'd projected my internal reality into a vision.

Then Mac was standing beside me. "Millicent, look who's here."

Had I willed him there? Summoned him?

"Hello, Millie," Dad said. He's the only one who calls me Millie. Then: "Well, this is some predicament you've gotten us into." Like in the old Laurel and Hardy movies. He's got a sense of humor, my dad. Only right then, it didn't match the worry in his eyes.

He came to the side of the bed. Mac stepped away. Dad leaned down and kissed me. I reached up and put my arms around him and hugged him for dear life. It was like he'd never left. I tried to sit up, but he wouldn't let me.

"You rest," he said. He pulled a chair over to the bed.

"How did you know?" I asked.

He gestured toward Mac. "Your brother called me."

So, my dad was probably within a couple of hours of us. "Did you fly in?"

"Sure did."

A couple of hours air time. He had his own private plane.

He talked. He held my hand. He stayed for almost an hour before the nurse said he had to go.

"You gonna stop *home*?" I asked.

He said no, he had an early morning meeting and had to fly back that night. When he said good-bye, I cried and he wiped the tears with his big, gentle hands. Then he kissed me again, said he had a contract soon in Boston and he'd fly Dexter and me up for the weekend.

"Mind your brother," he said. Then he walked out into the hall with Mac. I cried some more, silently, while he and Mac spoke in low tones out in the hall. My dad's such a good-looking man—broad shoulders, confident walk, take-charge manner. And he's still got those curls, though they're gray now.

Finally Mac came back in and told me to stop crying, how it wasn't good for my head.

"There's nothing in there," I said. "They did an MRI and told me."

He laughed. "You're okay, kid," he said.

"I hate my stupid family."

"Sure you do."

"All of you. I hate all of you."

"Right."

"Why can't we be like normal people?"

"There aren't any normal people. Take my word for it."

"I love Dad so much," I told him. "Why can't I have a dad like other kids? What have I got? You."

"Yeah, well, life ain't fair," he said.

Then I looked at him and saw the torn-up look in his eyes, the confusion. And I felt bad. "How is Darla? Did you ask?"

"In recovery. They were able to save her leg. But she won't be dancing at that bar anymore."

"Because of the leg," I said.

"No, because the township is passing an ordinance to close it down."

"Know what Naomi said?"

"What?"

"She said you were seeing Darla."

He kept a poker face.

"Are you?"

"In a way, yes."

I got a pain in my head. "I thought you and Carol were going to get back together. She asks about you every time I go for piano lessons."

"I thought so, too. But it might take more time."

I was confused. "So Darla's just temporary?"

"Not that it's any of your business, but Darla's a friend."

I knew when to back off. "Know what else Naomi said?"

He sighed, and sat down on the edge of my bed. "I can't wait to hear."

"Darla drinks holy water from the church. Says it keeps you from getting pregnant."

"Well, she may have made an important scientific discovery."

"And Naomi says that Martha isn't really buried in the churchyard. That she was cremated, and her ashes are in a vase in Mom's room."

He had taken my hand on the bedsheet. "That so?"

"Yeah, that's what she said."

He sighed heavily. "That girl sure does have an imagination. She'll probably grow up to be a fine writer someday. You can say you knew her when she ran around in her mother's ragged wedding gown."

"Is it true, Mac? About Martha?"

"Of course not. Anything else we can clear up now so you can get some sleep?"

I nodded. "Does Daddy have another woman?"

"I don't ask."

"Why?"

"He doesn't ask me. We respect each other's privacy."

Fresh tears came to my eyes and started down my face. "I wouldn't be able to stand it if he did."

"You'd be surprised at what we can stand in this world."

"I wanna go home."

He wiped the tears from my face with his fingers. "You will. Tomorrow. Just get some sleep now. I have to leave. This isn't good for you, hear me?"

It took a few minutes for me to stop crying. He held my hand the whole while. "You want anything?" he asked.

"I want Mom and Dad back together."

"That's the whole universe on a silver platter. Nobody gets that," he said. "You gotta learn to take a star at a time and be glad for it."

He kissed me on the forehead, real gentle like. And I have to tell you, I almost started crying again. Because there I had it. One star. And don't think I didn't know it. I'm not that stupid. Sure, I've got a rich, handsome dad who flies in on a silver plane and leaves. And who's left to clean up the mess? Mac. And Mom, who's grateful for whatever little bit of the mess he's left her.

But I still love my dad. God, I do. So much. I wonder if there's something wrong with me?

"Pick you up tomorrow," Mac said.

Chapter
Five

B efore we left the hospital the next day, Mac went with me to see Darla, who was half out of it, in her bed, still groggy from surgery the day before to save her leg.

She was hooked up to a couple of things that beeped, and she didn't look like a club kid. In the blue and white hospital gown, her face without makeup, her hair tied back, she was just a pretty girl in a bad way.

"Hello, Mac," she whispered.

They exchanged hellos and she managed a smile at me. "They saved my leg," she said. Then she gave him a special look, for all of her grogginess. "Won't be doing any more dancing for a while," she told him.

He told her about the place soon being closed down, anyway. "You've better things to do than that, Darla." Then he told her they'd gotten the man who'd hit their car. Not to worry. He'd pay.

She smiled again before closing her eyes, and I wondered if there was anything between them, or was Naomi blowing smoke out her ears. It was kind of confusing. Not for Mac or Darla, I could see that. They had it sorted out. It was confusing for me. There was magic in the world, I decided, that had nothing to do with the psychic, nothing to do with special powers. I wondered if I'd ever be tuned in to it.

In the car on the way home, Mac took a different route, once we got back into Glen Laurel.

"Where we going?" I asked.

"Just want to take you someplace for a minute. Are you up to it? Feel okay?"

I said yes and leaned back in the seat, feeling safer than I had in a long time. I'd come through a crisis. I'd been under Mom's protective powers, and they'd worked. I was in the car with Mac, who was being, all around, gentle and considerate this morning. What more could I want?

I was a little surprised when we pulled up in front of St. Sebastian's, the Catholic church. I looked at him questioningly.

"What are we doing here?" I got scared for a minute, thinking he'd found out about the Virgin Mary's toenails.

He unbuckled his seat belt, got out, and came around to open my door. Nobody was around. I got out. He gestured to me and I followed.

He looked out of place in his navy blue pants with the gold stripe down the side, and his glaring white shirt. He walked ahead of me, through the wrought-iron gate to the graveyard. Overhead, birds twittered. On the road, cars whizzed by.

He turned once. "Come on."

He knew where he was going, and so did I then. I made my way past the gravestones. Some had flowers in front, some didn't. And then Mac stopped, at a small marble angel on top of a gravestone, under a tree.

The stone said: MARTHA MACCOOL, BELOVED DAUGHTER AND SISTER. And it gave the dates.

I've had to study enough religions in my training to know that in all of them, death is not regarded as a finality, but just a part of the cycle of birth, death, and rebirth.

I know all the folklore about death, how in Somerset, England, they once believed that if you were dumb enough to linger at the church gate at midnight on Halloween to watch for the apparitions of those who would die in the coming year, your fate was to become a "churchyard walker" after you died, guiding the dead.

All of that was fine with me. But I didn't like being here any more than anybody else at that moment. Even with Mac, who was wearing his gun.

Then all of a sudden he knelt down in front of Martha's stone and crossed himself.

I'd never seen Mac pray. I didn't know what to do. It wasn't a normal sight, seeing a tall, muscular guy wearing a gun, kneeling and praying. It jolted me.

I looked away, across the headstones. Then, from the corner of my eye, I saw him cross himself again and stand up and motion me to where he stood.

I went to stand beside him. He put an arm around my shoulder. "She's here," he said. "She isn't cremated."

I nodded dumbly.

"You want to go with me to the rectory," he pointed to a neat brick building next to the church, "and ask Father Wisniewski? He officiated at her funeral."

"No," I said quickly. I didn't want to go anywhere near the rectory with Mac, so he and Father Wisniewski could start in talking about the "vandalism" of the Virgin Mary. The priests had carried on enough about it from the altar for the past two weeks.

"I personally saw Martha put in the ground. I promise."

"Okay," I said. Mac slipped his hand from my shoulder.

"I should have brought some flowers," he said. "Mom frequently does. I do, too, on occasion. So does Maddie. But with all that's been happening . . ." His voice trailed off. He started to walk away. "Stay a minute," he said. "You can visit and know your sister is here."

I watched him walk back to the car. No she isn't, I thought. Her spirit is at the river, in my secret place. But I knelt, the way I knew he wanted me to, and crossed myself and pretended to pray.

I didn't know what I was supposed to say. So I said a quick prayer for Darla, lingering long enough to appear respectful, then crossed myself again and got up and walked to the car, where he was waiting. The door was open. He was leaning his arms on the top of it.

"Listen, if Maddie bothers you about Dad coming to the hospital, you refer her to me. Okay?"

I hadn't thought about that. It was just what Maddie would do. "Yeah, thanks, Mac."

"Mom doesn't know. If she asks, you tell her the truth, of course. But if she doesn't, leave it be."

"Sure," I said.

"Take it easy today when you get home. Rest a while. Head hurt?"

"A little," I admitted.

"Take those pills the doctor gave you."

"They make me woozy."

"They're supposed to, so you rest."

I thought of the Percocet Naomi had offered me. Wow, he'd have a hissy fit if he knew about that.

Mom didn't ask if Dad came to the hospital. She had a cake made for my homecoming. She was just so glad I was okay. But not my sister Madeleine. She came over that same afternoon, sniffing around like an Irish wolfhound. "I'm so glad you're all right, sweetie." She kissed me.

She wants something, I told myself. Not that she wasn't usually nice to me. She was wearing black, her "widow's weeds" she calls them. I know she isn't still in mourning for Spencer. She just knows that, with her red hair, she looks good in black. Long flowing skirt, sandals, halter top.

Mom and I were having a piece of the cake she made. Mac had left.

"I thought I'd take you shopping for sneakers, the way a good big sister should. That way, you'll get there safely." She stood in the bright kitchen, smiling. It was her day off.

She needs kids, I thought. She needs to be married again.

"Not today," Mom said. "Mac wants her to rest. Why don't you two go into the great room and talk? Take some cake and coffee, Maddie. Millicent, it's time for your pill. I've got to rush out on an errand. Maddie, will you stay till I come back? I won't be long."

Maddie said she would. I took the pill and settled on the couch in the great room, wishing Mom had left me alone. I'd have been fine.

"How much did Mac give you for sneakers?" Maddie asked. No fooling around with her. She cuts right to the chase.

I told her and she got miffed. "You'd think, once in a while, with all his money, Daddy'd give something to me."

"C'mon, Maddie. Mac said when you were my age, Dad spoiled you rotten."

She lighted a cigarette. "Since he got wind of the fact that I'm dating Dennis, he's stopped. Says he's not going to underwrite another bad marriage. He doesn't like Dennis. Met him once. Can you get the unfairness?"

I could see Dad not liking Dennis. And Maddie was a spendthrift. She went through money like it came from a magic pouch.

"It isn't as if I'm not saving to buy into the salon," she said. She was in a sour mood, and I felt guilty for having a hundred dollars for sneakers.

"Daddy came to the hospital to see you, didn't he?"

"You'll have to talk to Mac about that."

"Boy, he's got you trained. Don't you ever want to break out and go against him?"

"Leave Mac alone, Maddie," I said. I sounded tired, because I was.

She was always trying to catch me in a lie so I'd lose my Power. She was jealous that I had it and she didn't anymore. Not only because she'd used her Power, but because afterward she let her magic lie fallow, and you can't do that or you'll lose it.

"All right, I'll lay off your precious Mac. I've got other things on my mind, anyway. I had a fight with Dennis."

"I'm sorry."

She sank back in the couch cushions. "All I want him to do is expand the shop. Doesn't he see how the new-money people are coming here? He said no, not yet, he doesn't want to overextend himself. After all, he isn't the only shop in town. People are starting to go to Shear Pleasure down the street."

60

She slipped off her shoes and put her bare feet up on the coffee table. Her toenails were bright red. "We argued. I called him stupid. Especially when he won't take me in as partner and take my money. Now I feel so bad. Would you do some damage control for me, honey?"

"What?" I asked.

"A spell for lovers. You know, one of those good ones Aunt Melanie taught you."

"I can't promise it would work. I haven't tried any yet."

"You could try."

"I'll think about it," I said.

She didn't speak again for a while. Puffed on her cigarette, sipped her coffee. Then she looked at me. "I hear from Naomi's mother that her father is getting out of prison soon," she said.

I shrugged.

"Look, do me a spell and I won't tell Mac. You don't think he's gonna let you be friends with that kid once he hears it, do you?"

She was blackmailing me. "I said I'd think about the spell, Maddie. You don't have to threaten me."

"I'm not threatening. Since when do I threaten you?" She reached out and hugged me. I let her, though I resented it big-time.

"Do you think Mac knows that Jimmy Beringer is doing drugs?"

Now she was really treading on me. This involved Dexter. Jimmy Beringer lived next door in a sprawling ranch house set back in the woods. He was a senior in high school, a star football player, and he'd taken Dexter under his wing, teaching him. His dad traveled a lot, and even when he was home he and Jimmy's mom hardly talked.

Maddie was going after Dex. I was very protective of Dexter. "We've known the Beringers all our lives, Maddie. Mom and Jimmy's mom are friends."

"You think that would matter to Mac?"

I knew it wouldn't. "Jimmy isn't taking drugs," I said. I didn't know for sure, but I had to say it.

Jeez, drugs. And Mac on a regular campaign against them.

"Then he's selling, which is worse."

I sighed. "Maddie, I said I'd think about the damned spell, so lay off and get out of my face about it." I moved as far away from her on the couch as I could.

"Oh, honey." She moved over to me. "I didn't mean it that way. I'm just inquiring about your and Dexter's lives. I'm interested. You think Mac is the only one who cares? I mean he may be your guardian, but I'm your big sister!"

She fussed with my hair where it touched my shoulders. "Do you know how pretty you are? Tell you what, you come on down to the salon tomorrow and I'll do your hair for school. We could lighten it a little."

"Mac won't let me dye my hair."

"Highlights. It's not dyeing. It'll look like the sun streaked it. He couldn't complain about that. Come on, honey."

I shrugged. "All right. But you've got to stop threatening me."

"I'm not threatening you. Did I tell Mac that you and Naomi made a blood promise to be friends forever?"

"Who told you that?"

"Her mother," she said airily. "She saw the cut in Naomi's palm and asked about it. And here." She grabbed my hand

and turned it palm side up. "There's your scar. Did I tell Mac that?"

I pulled my hand away. "Don't."

"C'mon." She put her arm around my shoulder. "Let's be friends and do some real girl talk."

Oh God, did I have to? My head was getting woozy.

Chapter Six

I have to confess, I like going to the hair salon. Mom says that when people lay their hands on you in a helpful gesture, it's healing. I like being fussed over. Who doesn't?

I also like listening to the chatter that goes on there. When I'm being worked on, my ears are wide open. And if I don't feel like listening, it's a good place to relax and get rid of my dysfunctional thought forms.

When I went the next day, Dennis was there. I think he's a great hairdresser, but he's a bit of a wuss. Aunt Melanie says there are people who are terrific at what they do, but they should never be in business, and I think Dennis is one of these.

Maybe he needs my sister's business head, after all. What she sees in him, I don't know. He's on the chubby side and has a baby face. But he's nice to me. He always teases Maddie about me, saying things like: "You better watch out, she's gonna be better-looking than you soon."

And when I make sure to sweep up my own hair or nail clippings because a person could use them to put a bad spell on you, he doesn't mock me.

"Good thinking," he says. "I wish all my customers thought like you."

At least six times in the past he's remarked on my hair, saying how shiny it is. "What do you use? Some secret formula?" he asks. He knows about our family and the magic, but I don't tell him a thing. And I've warned Maddie not to, either.

Mrs. Carlson was there, Naomi's mother. First thing I did, of course, was inquire after Darla.

"She's doing better, thanks, Millicent. And you thank your brother Mac for being so kind to me at the hospital the other night."

"I will."

She told me then that when Darla was discharged from the hospital, she would have to go into rehab. "I hope my insurance covers it," she said.

Madeleine painted highlights into my hair and put foil on and then left me next to the customer Mrs. Carlson was working on. I listened.

"I think he might show here in town," Mrs. Carlson was saying about her husband. "Though I hope not. I swear, I have no love for that man, what he's put me through."

"What if he comes to your house?" her customer asked.

"I've already told him no way. If he wants to see Naomi, he can pick her up and take her out to eat."

Talk about dysfunctional thought forms. But I was worried about my highlighting by then. When Maddie had painted it on, it looked like I would be bleached blond in those sections. But she said not to worry. And she was right. When she washed my hair, then did a trim and blew it dry, it was shiny and bouncy, and those highlighted streaks did look like they were from the sun.

I swept up the cuttings from my trim, and everybody said how nice I looked.

"You have great hair to begin with," Dennis said. "I've often remarked to Maddie. You people have a water softener at home?"

I shook my head no and gave Maddie a look because she was about to open her mouth and tell how I wash my hair in the wild water from the stream that runs through Mom's basement.

Mom says it's sacred water. Maddie is half convinced it is, and the other half of her doesn't care if it's dragon's blood. She's long known what it can do for hair and has bugged Mom for about a year now to bottle and sell it. Mom says no.

I wanted to get home. I needed to talk to Dexter. He'd be home from football practice soon. After what Maddie had hinted about Jimmy Beringer, I was worried about Dexter.

And I needed to help Mom. She was heading up the committee for the haunted house on Halloween again that year. That house was a big deal in our town. Mom and Mac had both come up with the idea a couple of years ago.

Give the kids a place to go after trick-or-treating on Halloween and it'd save grief all around. Especially the teenagers, who all wound up at house parties that ended up pretty wild sometimes, with the neighbors calling the police.

Mom used her connections as one of the old-time people who knew everybody and served on a lot of charitable committees, and got use of the old Meeker place out on Darah Road. The proceeds from the admission price went to the schools, for computers.

I left the shop and walked through town and up the hill.

It was a fine day in August. More like September, which I couldn't wait for. I hate August, the month of St. John's beheading and the Feast of the Hungry Ghosts. I know it's also the month of the First Harvest, but it's usually too humid and goes on forever.

Maybe I'd start making my ancestral cakes when I got home. I'd offered to make them for the haunted house on Halloween. I had to make at least six dozen, so I figured I'd start early and freeze them. Maybe I'd take a batch to Darla at the hospital. Yeah, that was a good idea. I still felt guilty about her being so torn up and her friend having the broken ribs and me getting off with nothing.

Of course, I'd protected Naomi with my talisman. But still.

"My, your hair looks pretty." It was the first thing Mom said when I walked in the door.

I smelled something cooking. "What are you making?"

"Lasagna. I'm bringing some over to Mrs. Carlson. Poor thing's been practically living at the hospital when she's not at work."

I kissed her. "You're a good person, Mom. Is Dex home?"

"Upstairs in his room."

I started out of the kitchen, then stopped. "Mom, did you tell Dex what you told me?"

"No. Mac said he would, if I wanted him to. I think I want him to. With you, it was different. The Power and all."

I ran from the room and upstairs.

Chapter
Seven

"Hey, Dex," I said. "How was practice?"
"Okay."

His room was a mess, as usual. Dex is sloppy. But still, I like his room. He has one of those lights that has water inside that swirls in different colors, posters all over the place of his favorite sports stars, a whole wall of old Pokémon cards, and another of Hess trucks. He's got all Mac's old Hess trucks, too.

I long since got rid of my ponies with the pink and purple hair, my Barbie and Ken dolls, and my Beanie Babies. In my room, besides my dream catcher, SPIDER, black cauldron, and Book of Shadows, I've got a copy of the *Witch's Almanac* and *Halloween Cookery*, also books on bird totems, animal-speak, and creative visualization.

Dex didn't look at me. A bad sign. And I knew what it was about. Sure, there was a karma between us, but Dex had feelings.

"How's Jimmy?"
"He's good."
"Did you hear? Naomi's father is getting out of prison."

"Yeah? Well you better stay away from her, then. Or at least not let Mac know you're hanging around with her."

"Mac's known it all summer."

"Yeah, well, things change."

In medieval language, he'd just thrown down the gauntlet. I picked it up. "I think maybe you better not let Mac know you're so tight with Jimmy, either, Dex."

He was sitting on the end of his bed, eating a sandwich and chips. He wiped his mouth with his hand. "Oh? Why's that?"

"I don't know if there's anything to it, but Madeleine said he's doing drugs."

"Madeleine also said Dad came to see you at the hospital. How come you didn't tell me?"

We stared at each other across the room. I know Dexter's sullen look, and not to mess with him when he gives it. In that way, he's a lot like Mac.

When he's not being sullen, he has this very sensitive mouth. He's so handsome.

But this was bad, Dad coming to see me and not stopping to see him.

"I had nothing to do with it, Dex. Honest."

"He always worries about you more than me."

"That's not true. He asked for you."

"Big deal."

"Dex, I'm sure if you got hurt he'd be there for you. Anyway, look at you and Mac. You think I don't envy the way he's so loose with you? Always high-fiving and pretending to get you in a hammerlock, you two pushing each other around? And I know you talk about girls on weekends when you go there. Mac doesn't act like that with me."

He swallowed what was in his mouth. "You're a girl."

"Well, he used to swing me around and let me sit on his lap."

"Yeah, when we were about eight. Jeez, give the guy a break."

"Dex, you'll get hurt if Jimmy's doing drugs."

"He isn't."

"Then what did Madeleine mean? You know she hears everything in that shop."

He shrugged.

I persisted. "Dex, your psyche is opened up with drugs, but it doesn't close up properly after, so you're left psychologically open and vulnerable to alien influences."

He set down the plate, took off his sneakers, and threw them across the room. "Don't give me all that crap. I don't need it."

"It's what Aunt Melanie taught me." I knew he respected Aunt Melanie.

"Look . . ." He stood up and set his plate on his night table. "I don't need any lectures, Millicent. And as far as I'm concerned, you not telling me about Dad visiting is as bad as you telling a lie."

I reeled from that one. Tears came to my eyes. Was he hoping, too, that I'd get caught up in a lie so I'd lose my powers?

"That's not fair, Dex. You know I don't lie. You know I can't."

"I'd like to shower now, okay?"

"Okay, Dex." I backed out of his room. "Only, you know Mac'll be embarrassed if you're connected, in any way, with Jimmy and drugs. And as much as he bugs me, we can't let that happen, Dex. We're still family."

"Yeah, I know, I know."

I did a sneaky thing then. I slipped into Mom's room, after making sure she was occupied downstairs. One of her woman friends from one of her committees had stopped by. I heard them talking from the stairway landing.

Mom has a fireplace in her room, and lots of times on winter nights she invites me and Dex in to watch TV or talk. I remember when she and Dad used to spend their evenings there in front of the fire. She also has an old-fashioned dressing table, the kind with the large oval mirror, that she got from her aunt Melissa.

Mom and her sisters were brought up by their aunt Melissa and uncle Edward. He was a lawyer, a silent, studious man who was overwhelmed by a house full of women, Mom said. I think that's why Mom and her sisters are so close. And why Mom and Dad fell in love. They were both orphans.

First I went to the mantel and took down a vase. I peered in. Nothing! No other vases in the room, either.

So! Naomi had been blowing smoke out of her ears.

Next I went to Mom's old hope chest, where I knew the album was. I opened the hope chest and took it out. Quickly, I went through it. Some of the pictures were faded, but sure enough, I found what I was looking for.

Pictures of Martha.

Golden-haired fairy child Martha. On Mom's lap. On Daddy's lap. On Mac's lap, when she was six and he was seventeen. She'd been the darling of the family before Dex and I came along.

Suppose she hadn't drowned? She'd be my big sister now.

Would she be better at it than Maddie?

All our lives would be different!

I stared at the smiling, curly-haired little blond charmer. She'd wandered off and gotten herself drowned. And now we all had to pay. She was careless, and if she hadn't been, we'd all be different today.

Sitting there with the album in my lap, the sun pouring in shafts across the room, I heard, as from another world, the clink of cups and saucers from downstairs, the cry of a bird outside, Dex thumping around in his room down the hall.

And then I was out of time for a few minutes, suspended, in what I knew was a state between sleep and wakeful consciousness. I knew better than to fight it. I knew I should relax and go with the flow.

A serenity came over me. And I could feel a presence in the room with me. A presence I knew was Martha. I can't explain how it works. You just *know*.

I was sensitive to all sound, especially the small voice speaking inside me.

"I'm not in that cemetery where Mac took you yesterday. At least my spirit isn't. I'm in that spot by the river that you like. Where I drowned. And that's why you're so drawn to it.

"I've been waiting to contact you. I want to make up for everything. I know what I did was wrong, but I was looking for the singing maidens that guard the underwater city. The same as you've looked for them.

"I want to make amends, so my spirit can go to the next level. And I've chosen you to do it.

"So pay attention to your higher self. Forget your jealousy and envy of me. You are very loved in this family. I need your help. Be ready to give it when I ask. And I will be ready to make amends when the time comes."

"Millicent? What are you doing with Mom's album?"

I was dragged out of this state of warmth and comfort like a baby from the womb. I felt a jolt and then was aware of the room around me. And Dexter standing in the doorway, wearing sweatpants and a T-shirt, a towel around his shoulders, his hair still wet from the shower.

"You shouldn't be looking at Mom's album," he said.

"Why?"

He shrugged. "I don't know. I always thought it was private."

I got up from the floor and put the album back. "Don't tell," I said. "Please?"

"Sure."

We went back into the hall. Dexter looked at me. "You okay, Millicent?"

"Yes."

"You're up to something, I know you are. One of your experiments. Look, don't do anything weird, okay?"

"Of course not."

"But if you do, and you need any help, you can ask me. I'm not sore, okay?"

"Okay," I said.

I went for piano lessons that afternoon at Carol's house. That's how Carol and Mac met. He picked me up from lessons once, years ago, before he went into the FBI, before he was married.

Carol also teaches music at the high school. She's got a neat place, down the road from Aunt Melanie and Aunt Mercy, a Victorian. It's cream-colored with green shutters, and a porch that comes out in a semicircle in front and wraps around her windows. She kept the house after she and her husband divorced last year.

Her husband was one of those computer eggheads. Carol is tall and skinny and sane. The only magic she does is teaching kids music.

That afternoon I felt a little funny, seeing her. I wondered if she knew Mac was seeing Darla. I guess I was a little distracted.

She gave me lemonade and cookies. "Worried about starting school?"

"Yeah. I know I'm an oddity, 'cause I've been home-schooled. And because of the way everybody in town thinks about us."

She's heard all the rumors about us, but she treats me the same as anybody else.

"Know what, Millicent?" she said. "Those kids are going to be as nervous about meeting you as you are about them." She put her arm around my shoulders on the piano bench.

"Thanks, Carol."

"So? How is your brother Mac these days?"

"He's okay. Do you still like him?"

She smiled. "Maybe a little bit."

I felt a surge of joy. "If he asked you out, would you go?"

"Not fair," she said.

"All's fair in love and war," I reminded her.

She looked at me. "Promise you won't tell him?"

Damn, there it was again. A broken promise was as good as a lie. "Promise," I said.

"Yes. But he has to ask. Now remember, you made a promise."

"I'll remember," I said.

* * *

After that I went to Aunt Melanie's. She was overseeing a gardener who was putting in two rows of rosebushes. The bed-and-breakfast is on a grassy slope with a walk to the front porch, which has striped awnings and wicker furniture.

"Millicent! How nice of you to come see me. How are you feeling, dear? How's the head?"

"Fine."

"Want some tea?"

We went inside. The house was empty of customers, and her helper, Gina, was changing the beds and doing the bathrooms. We sat in the sun-filled kitchen.

"Do you have a problem, dear? Your aura is fractured."

"Yes." I could never fool her. I didn't want to. "I've known all summer that Naomi's father is getting out of prison. But earlier today, Maddie threatened to tell Mac if I don't do a love spell for her and Dennis."

"Your sister knows better than that. I'll speak to her about it. As for Mac, I think he knows about Naomi's father. He dropped by earlier, looking for you. Said if you came by I was to tell you to stop in his office this afternoon. I'm glad it's only about Naomi's father. I thought it was about your Power."

"Oh, jeez."

"Now don't worry. Just be your usual sweet self. You know Mac indulges you."

I looked at her. "Where have you been, Aunt Melanie? Mac does anything but."

"Just tell him how you feel. If she means a lot to you as a friend, state your case. Mac respects honesty," she said. "And try to see his position."

It didn't sound good. Not promising at all.

"Oh, listen, I've got a new boarder. Came last night. His name is Carlos Ramirez."

"Boarder?" I knew some businessmen stayed for a week, sometimes two, but she'd never referred to them as boarders.

"Yes, he's here for TRK, the computer company. He's very handsome, dark hair, mustache. He's from Mexico. TRK wants to start a plant down there. But there's something about him."

"What?"

"I don't know. I've got a feeling."

Aunt Melanie was always trying to read her boarders' auras, and by her own law of probabilities, soon thinking they were all extraterrestrials.

"Does this guy glow in the dark or anything?" I asked.

"Not that I know of, honey."

"Are you worried about him? Do you want Mac to run his license plate in the computer or anything?"

"Of course not. Now let's go outside. I want to show you how beautiful my roses are going to be. They're going to be yellow. What do you think of that?"

I told her. "Everybody needs yellow, the color of knowledge and logic. It encourages people toward rational thinking and it represents attraction and desire."

She put her arm around me. "I taught you that," she said.

Chapter
Eight

When Mac came home to stay in Glen Laurel, Dex and I were both card-carrying brats. We'd been spoiled by Dad, and Mom and the aunts wouldn't think of discipline. We were on our way to juvenile crime.

I was a fairy child, Mom said, who ran around in summer barefooted, hair to my waist, always going to bed late, eating what and when I wanted and playing tricks on everybody.

Dex was a regular spawn of the Devil, with a mouth on him that would have made the legendary Finn MacCool's hounds flee in terror.

We wouldn't wear seat belts in the car, we interrupted people's conversations, we ran wild in stores, and, of course, there was that business with the school bus with Dex.

Mac took us in hand. He read us the law of the land. He laid down the rules and told us what would happen if we didn't obey. And what we could expect from him if we cooperated.

The options were like the Brothers Grimm versus Walt Disney. We agreed to cooperate. Mac was a hero in our eyes. He carried a gun and rode around in a car with flashing lights, and everybody called him "sir." Dex and I went from kids with no dad to kids whose big brother headed up the whole police department. Our status in the neighborhood definitely improved.

He came with bragging rights. And he told us that if this thing worked out, he'd be there for us, always. He was over six feet and had broad shoulders, and when he hugged us, Dex and I were like Hansel and Gretel who'd found their way home.

As I rode my bike to town that afternoon, I tried to fix in my head my argument for being allowed to stay friends with Naomi. Mac was tough, a pain in the butt sometimes, but he always listened to my side of the argument.

I parked my bike outside police headquarters and locked it, because we may be an idyllic Otherworld here, but let's face it, not everybody believes in such stuff. I went inside. The dispatcher at the front desk knew me and said Mac was in his office doing paperwork. Which means he was on the computer.

I knocked and Sir Owain bade me enter.

"Hey," he said.

"Hey, yourself."

Finnian was on the floor next to his desk. "Can I pet him?"

He nodded yes, so I knelt down and patted the dog's head. He didn't lift it, but thumped his tail on the floor. He knew me. You have to be careful with K-9s, not approach them when they're working, not that Finnian was working at that moment.

I sat down in a leather chair and waited for Mac to finish his work. I looked at his awards on the walls. Mac finished what he was doing on the computer and leaned back in his chair. "Want a Coke or anything?"

"No thanks."

"What you been up to?"

"Had piano this morning. Went to see Aunt Melanie."

"How's piano?"

I knew he meant Carol. "She's fine."

"Don't get snotty. I meant it about piano. How you doing?"

"Carol says I'm almost ready for Carnegie Hall."

"Make fun of the piano all you want. You'll be happy someday that Mom made you do it."

I knew I was giving him sass, but I just wanted to stand up to him, like Naomi said. Not let him push me around. And, of course, Mac was up to it. Whenever Dex or I were snotty, he gave back. As if to say: If this is what you want, this is what you've got.

For a moment we both fell silent. "Well," he tossed a pencil onto the desk. "The happy talk is over."

"Yeah," I said.

"Now comes the serious stuff." He cleared his throat. "Look here, Millicent, about this girl you're friends with. What's her name again?"

"Her name is Naomi."

"Yeah, that's it. Naomi," he said softly. "No need to be fresh about it. I couldn't think of the kid's name for a minute. And by the way, I'm sorry, I should have asked about your head. How are you feeling?"

I felt ashamed. "Okay."

"I'm somnambulistic sometimes."

I'd have to look that word up. I didn't know what it meant.

He uses big words on occasion. He went to Columbia University in New York, then two years of law school, and taught at the community college while he was waiting to go into the FBI.

"Well, anyway, I'll cut to the chase here. I heard her father's getting out of prison and likely to return here. I think it's time you ended it with Naomi, okay?"

"You can't ask me to do that, Mac."

"I'm not asking. I'm telling."

"Well, you can't do that, either."

"Oh? You wanna tell me why not?"

"Look, I know you can. But I can't promise. And it isn't fair, Mac. You can give ultimatums to Dexter and he says okay. He can lie to you."

"If I find out, he's in trouble."

"You think you always find out?"

"Since when are you snitching on your brother? I thought you two were attached at the hip."

"I'm not snitching. I'm just trying to explain things. I can't lie, and you know it."

"Yeah." He grinned a lopsided grin. "I know."

"And so it's unfair, you binding me to a promise. Because breaking a promise is as good as lying."

He shifted in his chair. I looked down at my hands in my lap. He has these blue eyes that bore right into you. And his face—it can register anything so well. Surprise, anger, confusion. I mean, it's a great face, with a strong jaw, and you know you don't mess with this guy, but he's still a guy, and so vulnerable. That's one of the things Aunt Melanie taught me, how vulnerable men really are. I almost feel sorry for him, tough as he comes off.

"So don't ask me not to see her, Mac," I finished. "She's my friend. It isn't Naomi's fault about her father. I'm going to see her. And I'm not lying about it. I'm telling you up front."

"So what do I do? Let you run around with a kid whose father is getting out of prison?"

"I won't do anything wrong, Mac. You know that."

Underneath it all, under all the posturing we both did, he knew. He looked uncomfortable now. "All right," he said. "All right. You can stay friends. But look here, Millicent. I'll cut out a llama's heart and offer it to the rising sun to keep you and Dexter in one piece till you're eighteen."

"Only till we're eighteen?"

"You know what I mean."

"Most people don't know the llama is a semidivine animal in the Andes," I reminded him. "You're giving yourself away. A person would think you knew magic." Of course he did. He was taught by Mom and the aunts. And in this family, you learn it by osmosis.

He waved away the thought. "I'm trying to tell you I'll go to any lengths to fulfill my responsibilities. So watch yourself. I don't have to tell you how to behave, do I?"

I sighed. "No. But you will."

He didn't laugh. He leaned forward, across his desk. "Remember this. I got any reason to go after this guy, I'm going to. And I don't want to hear anything out of you if I do."

I fell silent for a moment.

"Deal?" he asked.

"Deal," I said. I know how much it took for him to say that. I got up. "Thanks, Mac."

"And you better not tell Naomi that, either."

"You better not tell Darla."

The look he gave was quick and fierce. His eyes were like night vision, seeing through me. "What is that supposed to mean?"

I'd gone too far. I smiled sweetly. "Just teasing."

"Mind your own business. And get out of here before I kick your butt."

I started for the door. "You ought to pay some attention to Dexter," I said, "if you don't mind my saying."

He looked up quickly. "What's up with Dexter?"

"Well, in between all the guy stuff you two do, that I'm not allowed to be part of, he needs attention."

"Do I detect some jealousy here? What guy stuff?"

"Oh," I said offhandedly, "the *Playboy* magazine talk, the hammerlocks, the high-fives."

"I don't read *Playboy*. Don't need it."

"Oh, ho! Pardon me!"

He blushed. "C'mon, what's up?"

"You were a football star, and all Dexter's got is Jimmy Beringer next door to give him some pointers."

His eyes sharpened. "He's been hanging out with Beringer?"

Did he know about Beringer? "I'm just saying, you ought to help him with football, is all."

"Yeah. Thanks. I've been meaning to but I got busy. Look, you're too old for me to throw around anymore."

"Don't be silly. I'm going now. The influences in here are disturbing."

He looked vulnerable, and confused, when I walked out the door.

Well, I'd stood up to him about Naomi, hadn't I? And won? Then why didn't I feel elated?

Chapter
Nine

Carol took me to school one day before it started, to show me around. "It's awfully big," I told her.

"Not like some high schools. It's actually small and cozy," she said.

"I can't imagine learning in a place like this. I mean, thought forms are ethereal substances. If you're paying attention, you can see them. They float through space and hover over people's heads. What will I do in a class full of hovering thought forms?"

She stopped midway as we were walking down the hall and looked at me. "Wow, that's heavy."

I blushed. "I'm sorry, I shouldn't talk like that. We're not supposed to make others feel uncomfortable."

"I think it's fascinating."

"Please, don't. Mac doesn't buy into it. And if you buy into it, he won't have anything to do with you. My mom's marriage was a disaster on account of magic."

"I know. Mac told me." She nodded slowly. "Okay, I won't say anything about this tonight, then."

"Tonight?" I grabbed her arm. "You got a date with Mac?"

"Yeah. He's taking me to the supper club over in Washingtonville." It was the next town over, even more artsy-craftsy than ours.

"Hey, right on. Old Mac broke down, huh?"

She shrugged. "It was me, more than Mac, who was hesitating. I wasn't ready to start seeing anybody again after my divorce. And he was decent enough not to push me. Your brother is a really nice guy."

I wondered where Darla fit into this, but didn't say anything. "C'mon, show me the music room," I said.

I wore a skirt and blouse to school the first day to please Mom. What a bummer. All the girls had on either shorts or jeans.

Well, I thought, I'm different, they all know it, so I might as well look the part.

My homeroom teacher was Mr. Lishinsky. He was half bald but not bad-looking. And he introduced me, right off, as the new girl. Some kids snickered. Others just stared.

"Just because Millicent has been home-schooled until now doesn't make her different," Mr. Lishinsky said. "I guarantee you that whoever home-schooled her brought her on more field trips, had her do more hands-on projects, and delved deeper into subjects than we do here in school. Am I right, Millicent?"

I had to answer. "Yessir."

"What field trips did you go on last year, for instance?"

I thought about my out-of-body-experiences, but I couldn't talk about them. "Washington, D.C.," I said, "all the museums. Same for New York and Boston, plus Plimouth Plantation in Plymouth, Massachusetts."

"See what I mean?" Mr. Lishinsky said. "And what kind of hands-on projects did you do?"

I knew that making a Babylonian devil trap wouldn't hack it here. Even though I'd labored hours over the terra-cotta trap and lettered the Hebrew words myself.

"I learned how to make a whole French meal in my aunt's kitchen," I said. "I learned about the process a book goes through before it becomes a book. I visited a publishing house in New York. I spent a couple of months as a volunteer in our hospital. And I worked in a soup kitchen around the Christmas holidays two years in a row."

There were still some snickers. "All right, this is an English class now," Lishinsky said. "Let's get to work. Very instructive, Millicent, thank you."

Dexter and I had made each other a promise. We'd leave each other alone in school. They didn't put us in the same classes anyway. I think for all of Mr. Lishinsky's we're-all-the-same-under-the-skin routine, they were afraid of us.

It occurred to me halfway through Social Studies that Dexter likely hadn't told his classmates he didn't have magic. Wow! Why hadn't it occurred to me before? Power is as much perception as reality!

If they thought Dexter had powers, it made him special. He probably wasn't saying he did and wasn't saying he didn't.

Well, I wasn't going to mess things up for him, that was for sure. Dexter deserved a little fun, too, didn't he?

At lunch I sat with Naomi, of course. She was in three of my classes. I noticed some girls looking at me. Then two came over, Meredith Finch and Elizabeth MacElroy. They were friendly but cautious. I could tell they wanted to ask me about my Power but held back.

Turned out what they really wanted was me on the school newspaper. I said I'd think about it.

"Snobs," Naomi said when they left the table.

"I thought they were kind of nice."

"So I suppose you're going to hang with them now?"

"I didn't say that."

"Just remember what I said. These kids are gonna want to be friends with you just because of your magic."

My first weeks in school went by in a haze. I joined the school orchestra. Dex made the football team, second string. He was happy.

Mom had four contracts to do people's houses for Halloween, and I helped her make some decorations. What with the haunted house in the planning stages, too, she was overextended now and had to use her lavender pillow to sleep well at night, and to take St. John's wort for stress. Aunt Mercy says it was sprinkled with the blood of John the Baptist.

Things actually went along pretty smoothly. Mac came over whenever he got a chance, and he and Dexter threw around the football outside. Mac even attended a few practices. It did a lot for Dexter, everybody seeing Glen Laurel's old football star watching on the sidelines, giving hints to the kids, and knowing he was Dexter's older brother.

I forgave him for a lot of things because he took my advice about Dexter.

And then, just as I thought we were getting it together almost like a normal family, it all began to come apart.

I came home from the library around noon on a Saturday to find Aunt Mercy and Madeleine helping Mom make her hanging witches. They were working on the floor in front of the big fireplace.

"Your mother has to give this a lot of thought," Aunt Mercy was saying.

Mom was upset about something. I threw my books down on a table, grabbed an apple from a bowl, and sat down to listen.

Sure enough, Madeleine was stirring the pot of trouble again. From what I got, she was bugging Mom again to bottle water from the basement to sell in Heads by Dennis.

"He's close to taking me in as partner, Mom," she whined. "The water would clinch it."

Mom was firm. "Water is one of the natural elements. We don't sell it."

"They do in supermarkets," Maddie argued. "They make a mint on it. And in all the fancy restaurants."

"Well, we don't," Mom said.

"But this is magic water, Mom! Can't you see how great it is for the hair? Everybody asks me what I'm using. I could make a fortune."

"All water is magic," Mom returned. "We don't want to anger the undines."

The undines are half-aquatic and half-human creatures that reside in all water. They look like fish with human torsos.

"Oh, Mom, I gave up on that stuff years ago," Maddie reminded her.

"Just because you squandered your wish as a teenager, then gave up on your magic," Mom said, "is no reason to ruin it for the rest of us. Why, I couldn't face myself if I sold that water like a snake-oil salesman."

"I really think we should take the water and have it analyzed," Maddie said. "Maybe it isn't magic after all, but just has exceptional properties in it."

"No," Mom said again.

Maddie was really mad now. "For God's sake, Mom, it works wonders on hair. Don't be such an innocent."

"Let me make you some hair-washing water," Aunt Mercy intervened. "I'll put aloe, cucumber, dulse, gardenia, lily, lotus, and willow in it."

"It wouldn't be the same. I want the water in the basement. You know I need the money, Mom. How could you deny me?" And with that she got up and stamped out the front door.

"Whew," Aunt Mercy said. "Sometimes I'm glad I didn't have children, Mehitable." Then she turned to me. "Sorry, Millicent, I didn't mean that for you."

"I didn't think you did," I said.

Chapter
Ten

A week after Maddie's little tantrum, I was home alone on a Friday night. It was raining pretty hard. Mom had gone to a meeting of the haunted house committee, and Dexter was at the movies with some kids from school.

Nothing's more depressing than rain in September, but I was nice and cozy in my room, reading, in bed. My cat, Caramel, was sleeping next to me. At about nine o'clock I heard the noise coming from way below, in the basement.

The darned ironmonger is fixing his muskets again, I thought. I put my book down. Wouldn't it be great to really see him? How could he hurt me? He was only a ghost.

I put on my robe and slippers and grabbed a flashlight and my SPIDER. Boy, the rain was really slashing against the windows. We'd have flooding soon, and then we'd be cut off from the rest of the world. I kind of liked that. But I worried about both Mom and Dexter, out in it.

Caramel blinked at me as I went out into the hall. We've got to get a dog, I thought. I went downstairs and to the door in the kitchen that led to the basement. At the top of the stairs I recalled the verse to banish all ghosts, in case this guy was in a negative mood: Should Latin, Greek, and Hebrew fail, I know a charm which must prevail: Take but an ounce of common sense, 'twill scare the ghosts and drive 'em hence.

Would it work if I needed it? I couldn't wait to find out.

There was a light on down there. Or was that from his forge? And he was banging away. Only it sounded like glass. I crept down the stairs and looked in the direction of the light. There was a figure there. But right off I knew this was no ghost.

This guy had no strong medicine. There was nothing in the air between him and me. No breeze or smell of flowers, not even decayed ones. There was no fire going, no forge, and he wasn't transparent. He was real.

He was near the rock over which the water gushed before it flowed in the stream. "Who are you?" I demanded. "What are you doing here?"

He dropped something and I heard smashing glass. He stood and turned.

Damn, it was Dennis, Madeleine's boyfriend, the hairdresser.

I stared stupidly. He had a drop light at his feet, and from its glow I could see a case of bottles. He was filling them at the stream. He was stealing our water.

"How dare you?" I demanded. "How did you get in here?"

He pointed to the cellar door. The house has one of those old-fashioned outside ones that open out of the ground.

"You're stealing water from my mom's stream," I accused. "I bet this was Maddie's idea, wasn't it?"

"Look, Millicent, this isn't how it looks. I was going to pay your mom. Honest, kid. Don't get mad."

"That outside door is locked. Did Maddie give you the key?"

"Honey, she told me about the water. Jesus, kid, can't you see the possibilities? We could get rich."

"Don't you kid and honey me, and stop your blasphemy." I made the sign of the cross. "You get out of here, now. I mean it."

He was coming toward me. "I always liked your hair," he said. "So smooth and shiny. Now Maddie finally told me what you and she use. Come on, honey." He put his hands on each of my shoulders. I smelled whiskey on his breath. Oh, God, I thought, he's drunk. And I remembered Maddie saying he couldn't hold his liquor.

"C'mon, honey, be reasonable," he begged.

I'd never known him to be a violent guy. Maybe he thought he needed booze to pull this off. I pushed him away and stepped back. "Stay away from me," I said. I was very authoritative.

It didn't stop him. I turned and ran up the stairs, fast. He followed. I felt him grab my robe, twice. I untied the belt and he pulled it off, one sleeve at a time, with me switching the SPIDER from hand to hand. I reached the door and closed and locked it.

Then I grabbed the key to the outside cellar door, set the SPIDER down, and plunged outside in the slashing rain. It soaked me through in the first two minutes.

I had to move fast. If he got mad enough, he could break down the door in the kitchen, although why he'd want to bring such trouble down on himself, I didn't know. I ran to the side of the house, knelt down, set my flashlight beside me, and locked him in the cellar.

He was trapped. I wiped the rain from my face. Damn

Maddie! She would stop at nothing to get her own way. I ran back inside, shivering, and picked up the phone to call Mom. She'd be at the old Little Red Schoolhouse, the town's first school, now used for meetings. I knew the number.

The phone was dead. I looked around me in a panic for a minute. Dennis started pounding on the other side of the cellar door. "Let me out, Millicent! You had no right to lock me down here. I mean it, kid. Let me out or you'll be sorry!"

Yeah, sure. What to do? I didn't want this creep banging and maybe busting through the door. Then I knew.

I went to the garage through the door in the kitchen. Good, Mom had left the smaller car. I opened it, and just as I thought, she'd left her car phone.

Brilliant, Mom, I thought, going out without your car phone on a night like this. But thanks anyway.

I called Mac's beeper number and waited. It took less than five minutes before the car phone rang.

"Hello?" I answered.

He was alert, waiting for trouble on a night like this. Well, he had it. "I'll be right there," he said.

He came in ten minutes, and I swear I was never so glad to see him. He came with Finnian, who started sniffing around the basement door, barking and whining.

Dennis was still banging on the door and yelling. Mac took one look at me in my soaked pajamas and looked like he was going to have a meltdown. My hair was dripping, I was shivering, and I must have looked pretty scared.

"He put his hands on you?"

I thought quickly. Mac would kill him. But there it was again, I couldn't lie. "Not in that way, Mac."

"In what way, then?"

"Just on my shoulders. He wanted me to let him take the water. I handled him. Don't worry."

He told Finnian to be quiet and the dog obeyed. "Shut up, Dennis!" he yelled through the door.

Dennis shut up, too, but not before recognizing Mac's voice. "Oh, God," I heard him say.

"Has he got a gun?" Mac asked.

"No."

"Go on upstairs and change. Don't come down until I say so."

I stared. What was this turning into? That was Dennis on the other side of the door. Dennis who did heads. Maddie was dating him. What kind of a world was this anymore? "What are you gonna do?"

"Go on, I said!"

I ran. "Okay, Dennis," I heard my brother say. "I'm gonna unlock this door. I want you to calm down, hear me?" Finnian stood, ready, waiting for one word from Mac. I paused on the landing of the stairway, listening. In a few minutes I heard a scuffle. I heard Finnian growl and bark, then Mac say, "Down, boy." Then I heard Dennis whining.

"You gonna arrest me?"

Mac read him his rights. Just like on TV. Then I heard them go outside. I ran upstairs into my room, tore off my wet pj's, and got into some dry ones. I threw a sweatshirt on over them, put on some warm socks, toweled my hair, then ran out onto the landing and waited.

"Millicent!"

I ran downstairs.

"What was this doing on the basement stairs?" He was

holding my robe, standing there, him and Finnian, looking at me and waiting for the answer.

There was no way to explain it that would make things any easier on Dennis. I sighed. "I was wearing it and running upstairs. He was chasing me. He grabbed it and I let him pull it off so I could get away."

He nodded grimly and set the robe carefully over a chair back. "You did good," he said. "I'm proud of you. Except, I wish you would have called me before you went down there. It could have been anybody down there. And anyway, this guy's drunk. No telling what he could have done."

I glowed at the praise. "Should I call Mom?"

"I'll call her from the car. Where the hell is Dexter, anyway?"

"At the movies with friends."

"Yeah, well, lock this door good. I'll leave Finnian with you until Mom gets home. I'll pick him up in the morning. What was this guy after?"

I told him about the water and how Maddie and Mom had argued over it. He mumbled a curse. "Magic or not, it's Mom's water and this guy's a thief. Goddamn, can't Maddie pick somebody decent?"

We looked at each other for a moment, both thinking of the improbability of the whole thing. Mac reached out an arm and I went to him. "Thanks," I said.

"First thing we do is get a dog," he promised. Then he went out. I locked the door and peered out the window, watching the car move through the slashing rain into the terrible night.

Chapter
Eleven

"C'mon, Dexter, we have to go downstairs."

"Why?"

"Because it's a family discussion. Mac wants us down there, and so does Mom."

"I'm gonna kick the crap out of that Dennis. He's nothing but a faggot, anyway. If I'd been here last night I'd have laid him flat."

I sighed. "Yeah, I know. But he's not a faggot, just because he's a hairdresser, Dex. That's a stereotype and it isn't fair. It's not nice, either. He just had a little too much to drink. His business isn't doing well and he's losing money and he thought the water could save him."

Dex got up from his desk where he'd been doing homework. "What's the sense in going down? Mom already said she wasn't going to press charges. This is between her and Mac."

But whenever we had a family confab, it involved everybody. And Dex knew it. So we went down.

Maddie was pacing back and forth in front of the big fireplace in which Mac had lighted a fire. Coffee and a pan of scrambled eggs, bacon, bread, and fruit were on the coffee table in front of it. Outside it was still raining on this Saturday morning. Maddie was smoking furiously, her long hair disheveled. She was wearing tight black pants, a black turtleneck, and boots. She looked as thin as Lady Fand, a breathtaking beauty from the Otherworld who was always having trysts with lovers. All Maddie needed was a band around her forehead and grapes in her hair.

"Oh, shut up, Mac," she was saying.

Mac sat in a chair. Mom, in a silk robe, was pouring coffee. Mac was looking none too pleased. I assumed Maddie was ready to put a spear in his heart for arresting Dennis.

"I gave him the key!" Maddie said. "It wasn't a robbery. But no, you gotta go play Kojak and arrest him."

"Kojak!" Mac laughed. "You're dating yourself, Maddie."

She ignored that. "For God's sake, what did he do? Did he hurt anybody?"

"He scared the socks off your little sister, if that means anything to you. And he put his hands on her."

"You liar! You damned liar! How dare you?"

"Stop it, both of you," Mom yelled, and she never yelled. "Now let's not be at each other's throats. Mac, did you manage to keep it out of the paper at least?"

"It wasn't on the police blotter," he said, "but I can't do that too often, Mom, to protect my family."

"I know. I know, darling. But you did right. The bad publicity could ruin his business."

"You're worried about his business, Mom?" Mac asked. "The guy broke into your house!"

"I told you," Maddie said icily. "He had some business losses. People are going to the other shop in town because they've expanded and modernized. I've been telling Dennis that he's got to, but he wouldn't listen. He's got a cash flow shortage. He had a few beers and came here to bottle some water. As for Millicent, he didn't think anybody would be home."

She turned and saw me, sitting on the couch next to Dexter. "Did you tell Mac he put his hands on you? If you did, you know it's a lie."

"I told him he put his hands on my shoulders, to try to convince me everything was okay," I said.

"Oh, sure!" she said. "And I'll bet you played that up good to your big brother, too."

"Millicent doesn't lie," Dexter put in.

"You be still," Maddie told him. "Nobody's talking to you. If you'd been here last night instead of gallivanting . . . And anyway, you're in enough trouble, if it ever comes to light."

"What's that supposed to mean?" Dexter challenged.

I got scared she'd say something about Jimmy Beringer and drugs. Jeez, that was all we needed now. She looked at Mac. "You want to go after trouble, you ought to look on your own doorstep."

"I've got a good relationship with these kids," Mac said. "If Dexter's in any kind of trouble, he knows he can come to me anytime." I loved him for that, I really did. "You got any tales to tell out of school, you talk plain, Maddie, or shut up."

She shut up. Dexter didn't. "If I'd been here, I'd have laid the guy flat," Dexter told her. "The damn fag."

"Dexter, hush," Mom said.

"You dare!" Maddie started for Dex, who got up from the couch and faced her, and for the first time I saw how he was as tall as she was, and how, because he was working out in school, he had muscles he'd never had before.

"Is that what they're teaching you in football?" Maddie asked. "To lay people out? I hope you're happy, Mac." She scowled at Mac, then looked again at Dex. "You say that again, football player," Maddie told him. "You dare."

"He's a faggot," Dexter said, staring right at her.

Maddie slapped his face. The sound was sharp and it must have hurt, because Dexter reeled, then recovered himself. I saw him clench his fists and saw Mom start toward them, but Mac was there first.

He took Maddie's arm, gently, and pulled her away. "Don't you ever touch these kids," he said firmly.

"Oh," she whirled on him. "And you don't, I suppose?"

"I've never touched them in anger, no."

It was true. Mac had never struck us. Maddie sat down, defeated, and started to cry.

Mom went to her, comforted her. Mac patted Dex on the shoulder, said something to him in a low voice, and Dexter sat down beside me again.

"I think we've all acted a little irrationally," Mom said. "Dexter, we've raised you better than that. I think you ought to tell Maddie you're sorry for that remark. We all know Dennis isn't gay, and if he were, we don't criticize."

"Tell her to say she's sorry," Dexter countered. "She hit me."

Mom looked at Mac, who looked at Dexter. "Do as Mom says," Mac instructed quietly.

Dexter said it. "Sorry," he mumbled.

Mom nudged Maddie. "I'm sorry, too," she gulped, wiping her eyes. "So where does this leave us?"

"I'm not pressing charges," Mom said. She looked at Mac.

"I'm sorry, I can't. It would destroy my family."

"He isn't family," Mac insisted.

"He could be," Mom said. "What then?"

"He should have thought of that before he came barging in here, scaring Millicent half to death. Doesn't that count for anything, Mom?" Mac appealed.

"Were you scared half to death, Millicent?" Maddie asked.

Everybody was looking at me. Next to me on the couch, Dexter moved his hand imperceptibly and touched mine. I knew what he wanted me to say. I knew what Mac wanted me to say. And there I was, torn.

And there was the truth, and I couldn't lie. I drew in my breath and let it out slowly. "Mac," I looked at him, "you said last night I shouldn't have gone downstairs without calling you first. Only reason I went was because I thought it was a ghost down there. I mean, I took my black box. I thought it was the old ironmonger, banging away. I know you all will laugh, but I hear him lots of times on stormy nights. And I just wanted to see him."

Nobody laughed. But I saw Mac hunch his shoulders forward and knew what he was thinking. Ghosts now. As if we haven't got enough.

The room was silent but for the ticking of the clock and the crackling of the fire. My whole family was staring at me.

I went on. "Then I saw it was Dennis. At first, I was mad. I thought he had a nerve, and I told him so. Then I saw he was drunk. I told him to back off and he wouldn't. That's when I ran up the stairs and he came after me. And that's when—" I gulped. "I was scared, yes. If I hadn't been, I wouldn't have run outside in the rain and locked him in."

I looked at the floor. Beside me on the couch, Dexter covered my hand with his and squeezed it, as if to give me courage. "I'm sorry, Maddie," I said. "But I was scared."

She glared at me, and I thought, I've just lost my sister. And I felt a pang of sadness.

"Well," Mom said, a little too cheerfully for me. And I think for Dexter and Mac, too. "I, for one, think it was a misunderstanding. If it went to court, Mac, and the judge heard Maddie gave him the key . . . " Her voice trailed off. "Well, I'm not going to press charges, son, I'm sorry. It would cause irreparable damage in this family and we've already had enough damage, don't you think?"

Mac didn't agree, I could tell, but he was never disrespectful to Mom. At least not in front of me and Dexter. He got up, put his cup down on the table, and signaled for me and Dexter to follow him.

We went into the kitchen. "I don't want to hear that you two gave Mom any trouble about this," he said.

We faced him solemnly.

"Or Maddie. Don't get on her. And no more talk about Dennis being a fag, Dex. I mean it. Do I have your promise on that?"

We promised.

"Why won't Mom press charges?" Dexter asked.

Mac shrugged. "Things happen in families that aren't right. You gotta accommodate yourself sometimes. Mom's been through a lot. Holding her family together means more to her than anything. If she presses charges, she knows she loses Maddie. She already lost one daughter. She can't lose another."

"That was sickness," Dexter said.

Mac sighed, and closed his eyes for a moment. "Get your jacket and come on with me, Dex. I gotta go down to the station."

"Millicent, too?"

"No, there's things you and I gotta talk about."

"I didn't do anything," Dex said.

"Not saying you did." Mac had his hand on the doorknob and winked at me. "Look after Mom," he said. "We'll be back later."

I knew he was going to tell Dexter about Martha and how she'd died. I didn't envy him. I only hoped Dexter wouldn't be mad at me because I found out first, is all.

Chapter
Twelve

Dex came home that night looking pretty stunned. We sat up late in his room, while the rain poured against the windows, and talked about Martha.

"What else don't we know?" he asked. "What are Mom and Mac keeping from us?"

"I don't think there's much more, Dex," I said. "And I don't think they're keeping things. I just think it's a matter of them wanting to make sure we're old enough to absorb it all."

"Well, I am," Dex said. "What about you?"

"Sure," I said.

"What a nice man he is," Aunt Melanie said of her new boarder, Carlos Ramirez. "And he must have a wife and daughters at home. Every time he comes in, he has more purchases in his hands for them. He enjoys his food, too. I do like a man who compliments you on the food. Well, dear, so how are things at home?"

We were in her front parlor. Breakfast was long over. From the kitchen came sounds of Gina doing the dishes. "Terrible,"

I said. "Mom's so upset with herself because she's not pressing charges. And upset with Mac because he wants her to. I wish I could do a spell and make damn Dennis into a warthog or something."

Aunt Melanie scowled. "Sit down, Millicent."

I knew what I'd said was wrong. I'm not stupid.

"What have I taught you?" she asked gently.

"I know, Aunt Melanie."

"I'm not sure you do. I thought I made myself clear, Millicent. Magic is not having influence over other people in the world. Our gifts do not enable us to change people and circumstances to our liking. They are mystical arts that help you to change the way you perceive things, that teach you to function in life as it exists."

"I know, Aunt Melanie. I was only letting off steam."

She sighed. "Tell me what you know."

"Ordinary people think that magic means forcing other people to do things. My personal Power won't work if I try to do bad things to others. I can't use my wish to destroy someone else. And I shouldn't use it to sing like Madonna."

"Good. And your everyday magical powers?" she asked.

"I can do spells to protect myself or someone else, to make life better, maybe even to get a guy to date me. But mostly my everyday magic is to help me find my place in the natural scheme of things."

"Don't you ever let me hear you say something like you did before," she said sternly. "I am responsible for cultivating your Gift, Millicent."

I promised. Then we practiced all the requirements for shape-shifting, she made me lunch, and I left.

I was going to the mall with Dexter. Mac was allowing us

to get a dog because of what had happened at the house. We weren't buying one at the mall, just looking.

Dexter wanted to get a greyhound from the Save the Greyhounds organization. Mom said she thought we should go to the town dog shelter and give some nice dog a home. I wanted something small that I could hold in my lap. Like everything else in our family, this was turning into a problem that needed a summit meeting to solve.

Mom dropped us off at the mall. We wandered around for a while, then went to the pet shop. We looked at the puppies, all yapping in their cages. Oh, they were so darling!

"Look at the pug," Dex said.

It was precious, with its pushed-in nose, big eyes, and frowning forehead.

"It comes with papers," a salesgirl smiled at us. "Do you like pugs?"

"Never thought much about them," Dexter told her.

She spoke to him, not me, the way all the girls did when we were out together. Dexter is so handsome and shy and self-conscious, he looks like a puppy dog himself sometimes, and all the girls want to take him in their laps and hold him. This one was definitely coming on to him. But Dex was so dense about stuff like that, he didn't know it. Or if he did, he was too shy to acknowledge it.

"They make great pets," she was saying. "They're wonderful with children, and they bark to let you know somebody's at the door." She unlocked the cage and handed the puppy to Dex, who then gave it to me.

She told him the price.

"A thousand dollars," Dexter said. "That's too much."

The girl nodded, put it back in its cage, then motioned for

us to follow her to the back of the store. "I've got something I want you to see," she said.

In back was a room full of crates and packages and shelves. And there, in a crate on the floor, was a pug puppy.

"Got some visitors, Sweetie," the girl said. And she unlocked the crate and handed her to us.

The puppy immediately took to licking our faces. "Why is she back here?" Dexter asked.

"We can't sell her," the salesgirl said. "She's got a virus in her eyes."

"Is she blind?" I asked.

"No," she answered, "and we're reasonably sure that medicine will cure it in time. We've taken her to the vet. Still, we can't sell her, according to American Kennel Club rules. But we can give her away, only not with papers."

Dexter and I took turns hugging and holding the puppy. When I held her, I felt the warmth of her body melt into my own and felt a moment of joy and peace and oneness with her. And when she looked at me, it was almost as if she was saying, I thought you guys would never come. I waited and waited.

My heart went out to her, alone in the back room with no hope of a home. Dexter and I looked at each other.

"What if nobody takes her?" Dex asked. "What will happen?"

"We'll give her to a place that does animal research."

"Do you think?" I asked Dex.

I didn't have to finish my sentence. "Yeah," he said. "But we have to ask him together."

"You want what?" Mac asked.

Mom had dropped us off at Mac's. He was on his back patio reading the Sunday papers.

"You gotta see her, Mac," I said. "She's so adorable. And sitting all alone in that cage in back of the store."

Mac shook out the paper he was holding. "I tell you two to get a good guard dog and you get an ant that can't see."

"Aw, c'mon, Mac," Dexter said.

He went on reading the paper.

"We haven't had a dog before this," Dexter said. "Now all of a sudden we've got to have a Finnian?"

"No." Mac looked at us each in turn. "I just thought that after the other night a good dog would help. I worry about the three of you there alone sometimes."

"She'll bark," I promised. "Alert us. That's all we need."

"Yeah," Dex said, "and if you want, later we'll get a real guard dog. This way we'll start small."

"Two dogs?" Mac laughed. "Good luck trying to convince Mom to allow that."

"If we convince her, can we have this one?" Dex asked.

Mac shrugged. "Oh, go ahead. Get your feet wet with this one, and if Mom agrees, I'll get you guys a real guard dog later. But you're responsible for her. Not Mom. Hear?"

"You gotta come with us," Dex said. "We can't do this without a grown-up. We need you, Mac."

Those were the magic words, and Dexter knew it. Mac grumbled about no peace on a Sunday to read the paper, but he came. He approved of Sweetie Pie, which was her real name.

Of course, the girl in the store flirted with him, too. Only Mac knew it. He gave us money for a crate, food, a leash, everything. I don't know who was happier, the dog, or me and Dex.

Chapter
Thirteen

Monday morning in school, Naomi was sashaying her tail all over the place, showing off new clothes.

"Mom saved her tips and never told me," she said. "How do you like?"

New jeans, new sneakers, sweater, backpack, even a leather jacket. All designer stuff, too.

"Wow," I said.

"Yeah. Is it all too, you know, over the top?"

"No, you look great, Naomi. I'm happy for you."

I was. It wasn't a lie. It was hard, seeing her sad because she didn't have what other kids had. And she'd been really down lately, since I joined the school newspaper and orchestra. But I couldn't keep myself from doing things because she wasn't a joiner, could I?

Miss Hardcase blew her whistle in front of the gym. "Millicent MacCool?"

Her real name was Miss Harbase. We called her Miss

Hardcase. I went to the front of the class, which was assembled for volleyball, wondering what I'd done.

"Didn't I say no jewelry in gym class?" She was holding the volleyball in front of her, as if for protection. Did this lady really fear me? I enjoyed the thought.

"I'm not wearing jewelry," I said.

"And what's that on your wrist?"

Because I'd given my amulet away to Naomi, Aunt Melanie gave me another one, a silver basket-weave bracelet with no clasp. I'd forgotten I had it on. "I never take it off," I said.

"Well, you're taking it off now."

"I can't."

"Oh, and why can't you?"

Everybody hated this woman. She favored the girls who were jocks and made the rest of us feel like misshapen people. The air around her was all misaligned. She had no fluid movement in her body.

But she hated me on a personal level. I could feel the negative energy coming off her toward me. I knew why. She was one of those people who was so superior, physically, that she feared anybody who might possess any other kind of power. She understood only physical power.

I'd promised Mom and Aunt Melanie I wouldn't flaunt my magic in school. So all I said was, "It doesn't come off. There's no clasp."

"It can be cut," she said.

"It was a gift."

"Sorry, MacCool." She gave a couple of bounces to the volleyball. "Either take it off now or go to the principal's office. I can't risk your catching it on something and getting injured. School rules. Now go."

I went. I knew what kind of a mess I was in now. I couldn't take gym if I didn't take off the bracelet. And you had to make up all the missed gym classes or you'd never graduate.

All I could think of on the way to the principal's office was the way Mac had told him "no special treatment" for me and Dex. And Mr. Rudolphi sure didn't cut me any breaks.

"You'll apologize to Miss Harbase, take the bracelet off, and go to gym tomorrow," he said.

"I can't take it off," I said.

He looked at me and sighed. "You going to push me, Millicent?"

Jeez, he even sounded like Mac. "I'm sorry, sir," I said.

He shrugged. "Okay, find a study hall for this period. I'll have to call your brother."

By the end of the day the whole school was abuzz, but not about me. Word was going around about some robberies in and around Glen Laurel.

There had been three over the weekend: a 1998 BMW stolen from the mall parking lot, a set of sterling silver servingware stolen from a house on Carter Road, and a firearm from another house in Glen Laurel.

I thought of Dennis and a thrill of fear ran through me. He wouldn't do something like that, would he? I knew Mac had released him from custody Saturday, after Mom refused to press charges.

Liz McElroy lived on Carter Road and told me after school that she'd called her mom, and the police were all over the place, questioning, looking for clues.

"That silverware set belonged to Mrs. Agren's great-grandmother," Liz said. "You know how she volunteers at the hospital? Mom says whoever stole it must have been watching her house and knew she wasn't home. She lives alone, you know.

"What are you going to do about gym?" Liz asked.

"Hope my brother is up to his ears with the robberies. He probably won't be home all night."

I walked home quickly. I had homework and I wanted to see the puppy, play with her. On the way up the hill a sports car stopped alongside me. "Hey, you know the way to the Lubbock place?"

I pointed up the hill. "Second left. You have to go in about two miles. It's real rural. Part of the road isn't paved."

"Thanks." He made as if to drive off, then looked at me again. "Need a lift?"

"No thank you." I felt a sense of fear. Where did I know him from? Dark hair, clean-shaven. I couldn't think. He wasn't a local. Maybe he was one of the robbers. The paper had said they thought there was a whole ring of them.

He started off. Great, I thought, I've just given directions to a robber. The Lubbocks were well-to-do, had horses and everything. But I memorized the license plate quickly so I could tell Mac. The car? Why hadn't I noticed what kind? I'm not good at cars. Green, British racing green, and some kind of sports model. Jeez, I thought, maybe we should have gotten a real guard dog after all.

I was wrong about Mac. Oh, he was up to his ears in the robberies, all right. And he did work all night. But the next morning I was just coming back into the house for breakfast after walking Sweetie Pie when he drove his chief's car into the driveway, raising dust. He got out, picked up the morning paper, and nodded to me as we went in the side door. I unleashed Sweetie. Mom had just called Dex down to breakfast.

"Mac!" She was breaking eggs into the pan. "You're just in time. Want some breakfast?"

He shrugged and kissed her cheek, threw the paper down on the table and sat down. "Coffee'd be good right now."

"Millicent, serve your brother some coffee," Mom ordered.

I did. Mac didn't look at me. Bad sign. Dex came into the kitchen, petted Sweetie Pie and sat down. "Hi, Mac."

"Dex," Mac acknowledged. But still no word to me.

Mom served everybody eggs. I did the toast. "Did you work all night, honey?" she asked Mac.

He grunted.

"Any clues?"

"Some." He cradled his coffee cup in his hands, warming them. It was a brisk morning. I'd noticed the outside thermometer read only fifty. Mac was wearing a dark blue windbreaker. He zipped it open but didn't take it off, and when he moved, I saw the gun he wore, inside it. I never saw his gun without getting a jolt. He wore it so casually, and it always made me know there was more to my brother than I knew about. A side to him I didn't want to know about. How can you so casually wear something that can kill people?

We ate. Mac talked some about the things that had been robbed, but Mom didn't push. She knew he couldn't divulge anything. He asked Dex about football, and Dex kept the conversation going.

I could tell Mom knew something was up with Mac. The air was so heavy and the vibes so bad, I think even Dexter knew it.

Finally, when we were near finished, Mac looked at me. "Did you tell Mom?" he asked.

"What?"

"C'mon, Millicent. About the trouble you're in at school."

"No." I looked down, shamefaced.

"What trouble?" Mom asked.

Dex knew, but he hadn't told.

"You don't tell your mother?" Mac asked. "Keep her in the dark about such things, do you?"

Oh, jeez.

"Tell her," he said.

So I did. Mom looked apprehensive, then disappointed. "We should have thought about the ramifications of such a bracelet, Melanie and I," she said.

"It's not your fault, Mom," Mac said. "Millicent knows right from wrong. What are you going to do about it?" he asked me.

I shrugged. "It's stupid, having to take it off. It's my amulet. What do you think kept me safe the other night when Dennis was in the basement, chasing me and practically pulling off my robe?"

Mac wasn't buying it. He got up and went to the drawer where Mom kept small household tools and took out some kind of shears or something. He leaned against the counter and motioned me to him.

I got up from the table and backed off. "No."

Dex's eyes went big. Sweetie Pie sensed the danger in the air, and her curled pug's tail went out straight. Mom said, "What?" then caught on and said, "Oh, dear."

Mac just stood there leaning against the counter. "I'm tired, Millicent," he said. "Been up all night, and I have to get to a new crime scene. I'm damned if I'll go over to that school and have a conference with Rudolphi or anybody about anything as all-fired stupid as this. Now let's get it over with."

"Mom," I appealed, "you can't let him."

Mom stood up and came over to me. "Honey, now listen, Aunt Melanie will make you a new amulet."

"I don't want a new one. I want this!" I looked at my brother. "It's not stupid! What do you think protected me when that creep stopped his car on the road yesterday and asked directions to the Lubbock place, then offered me a lift?"

Mac's eyes narrowed. "The Lubbock place?"

"Yes."

"It was robbed last night. What'd he look like?"

"You cut off my bracelet and you can go to hell."

"Millicent!" Mom scolded. "For shame, talking like that to your older brother."

Mac cut me a look for the sass that let me know I'd hear about it later, all about how I could say anything I wanted to him in private but not mouth him in front of anybody else. Then he came across the room, put his hand on the back of my neck and led me gently to sit down. He sat opposite me and picked up my wrist.

"I told you not to bring this magic stuff into school, didn't I?" he said.

I cried while he did it. I watched the shears cut through the beautiful basket weave and felt my veins shedding blood. My shoulders shook and tears came down my face. After a moment the bracelet came off. He set it on the table.

"You wanna tell me now," he asked softly, "what the creep looked like? Or you wanna withhold information?"

113

I wiped my eyes and nose with my hand. I blubbered. Mac gave me his handkerchief and I blew my nose. He waited until I was finished.

"Green car," I said.

"What kind?"

"British racing green. Some kind of a sports car. I don't know."

"Sounds like the MG we saw outside the school yesterday," Dex offered.

"See who was in it?" Max asked.

Dex shook his head, no.

"He was dark-haired," I said, "but clean-shaven. I got the license plate number." I gave it to him.

Mac stood up, put his hand around my shoulders, bent over and kissed me. "Good girl," he said. "Thanks."

Then he looked at Dexter. "Tell the kids not to talk to this guy if he shows up around school again, okay? I'll alert school authorities."

Then he left.

Mom sent Dexter upstairs for his jacket.

"I hate him," I said.

"Hush. You don't."

"I do. Because he doesn't let you hate him. He doesn't even let you do that."

"He does have charm," Mom said. "And you know? It's as good as magic. In that way, I'd say he's just like his father."

Chapter
Fourteen

I sulked in my room for two days after that. I did my homework, watched TV, and played with Sweetie Pie. Dex knew
I was in a slump. He walked her and otherwise kept away.

One night I tuned in to the local cable network on TV.
The Town Council was meeting and they were questioning
Mac. Something about them voting on an ordinance to let
cops go into houses without being asked, if neighbors said
there was a drinking party going on and no adults at home.
Lots of counties were doing it.

Mac stood there and answered all their questions. They
asked him about the Constitution, trying to catch him, but he
told them that the Civil Liberties chapter in our state said it
was constitutional. "If the people vote for this, we'll do it, like
other townships are," he said. "You vote it down, we won't.
It's up to you."

I was so proud of him, talking about the Constitution and
how he and his force were public servants. Then I remembered how mad I was at him.

After two days of sulking I managed to come up with a
first-class migraine and a low-grade fever. Good, I thought,

I'm sick and it's Mac's fault. God, I was a brat. I couldn't believe what a brat I was.

Mom kept me home from school and called Aunt Mercy, then Mac. She handed me the phone in bed.

"How'd you manage to do this?" he asked.

"I worked on it," I said.

"Yeah, well if Aunt Mercy says, you go with her to the doctor today. No arguments."

"You gonna bust into kids' parties?"

"What do you care? You won't be at such parties."

"Kids in school will be asking."

"Mind your own business. You've got enough to mind." He slammed down the phone. Oh yeah, he was sore. And I knew why.

It wasn't as much the problem with the bracelet as with the fact that it proved I wanted my magic and wasn't going to give it up. I'd just as well as told him.

Both aunts came, fluttering around me. Aunt Mercy held an agate to my brow to get rid of the fever.

"What have you learned about shape-shifting?" Aunt Melanie asked.

I sniffed, then answered. "A shape-shifter can adjust her behavior to conditions around her."

"Exactly. We all must adjust our behavior to the situations life throws at us. According to need. We must learn to adapt to change. That is the cornerstone of shape-shifting, is it not?"

"Do we have to discuss this now?"

"Yes, we do. How do you expect to be ready to practice shape-shifting if you do not adjust to this?"

"He cut my bracelet off! My amulet."

"He had to, darling," Aunt Melanie said. "The school has

rules. I really think he was very nice about it. He didn't scold or punish, and he's all tied up with these terrible thefts in town."

"You always stand up for him, both of you. You coddle him and bring meals over to his house. You buy him new shirts, socks, and underwear and put them in his chest of drawers. You do spells for his love life."

Aunt Mercy laughed. "He's always been our darling, yes. He's very special. A knight if there ever was one."

"A knight!" I scoffed.

"He is, darling," Aunt Mercy said softly. "Who do you think the knights of today are? The people who, every day, put their lives on the line to keep order and peace. So, he drives a car with red and blue lights instead of riding a horse."

I said nothing.

"But you and Dexter are also special to us," she continued. "And even Madeleine. Do you know I stayed up two nights mixing special water for her and Dennis to sell in the shop? And they bottled it ever so prettily. And it's selling!"

"We spoil all of you," Aunt Melanie said. "It's our job. I know, I know." She patted my head. "You feel powerless. Well, you aren't. Don't forget, next week is your birthday. Your Power is due. But also, don't forget that we can withhold it for a while if you aren't ready."

"You wouldn't do that, would you?" I asked tearfully.

"We must know that you can adjust to the situation, stop moping, and shift your consciousness to align with the forces around you," Aunt Melanie answered.

"Definitely," Aunt Mercy agreed.

"I can," I promised.

"And remember," Aunt Mercy added, "that your brother

Mac is only a poor, vulnerable man, and you must be good to him. You show us by the end of the week that you can adjust, shift your energies to meet this trial, grow spiritually from it, and act nicely toward your older brother, and on Saturday you will do some shape-shifting."

I gulped. "For real?"

"I don't say things that I do not mean, Millicent," she assured me solemnly.

"I'm ready, you know. I've been studying the deer. I've been watching their movements in the backyard. I know how they act, walk, sniff the ground, chew, everything."

Aunt Mercy removed the agate and felt my brow. "Fever's gone," she said. "That powder I gave you should get rid of the headache soon, if you sleep."

"Good." Aunt Melanie stood up. "I think it would be nice if you made Mac a cake, though. Wouldn't it, Mercy?"

"Oh, yes," Aunt Mercy said. "Cake has always been a magical food. Think good thoughts about your brother while you're making it. Remember all the good things he's done for you. And put plenty of vanilla in it. Vanilla imparts peace and can help defuse tense situations."

"I have to make Mac a cake?" I asked dismally.

"Vanilla," Aunt Mercy said. "Plenty of vanilla."

"And remember, Saturday, but only if we approve of your behavior," Aunt Melanie said. "Pick a four-leaf clover at the hour of Jupiter before sunrise. You're in luck. Tomorrow is the first Tuesday of the new moon."

Then they were gone.

I made the stupid cake for Mac, and tried to think good thoughts about him as I made it. I remembered how, when

Dex and I were younger, Maddie used to tease us a lot, and Mac would always stop her. How he used to hold me and Dex both on his lap and read us stories. That was even before Daddy left.

I remembered how one Father's Day after Daddy left, the town had a father-daughter bus trip to a ball game, and I cried because I couldn't go. And Mac took me.

And what about just last year when Maddie hit me with a wooden spoon because I sassed her, and Mac scolded her and said, "Don't you know these kids have no father, Maddie? Do you know what that means? You and I, we had a father!"

I put plenty of vanilla in the cake. I made the icing extra sweet. Mac has a sweet tooth. I dropped it off in his refrigerator when he wasn't home and left a note: "It's fat free." Yeah, right. And when he called to thank me, I could hear the surprise in his voice. "I never expected this."

"Yeah, well."

"What's up?"

I could tell he was waiting for the punch line, for me to ask for something. "It's got arsenic in it," I said.

"Gonna put me out of my misery, huh?"

We talked for a bit. About nothing in particular. Then he asked, "Okay if I take the cake to work and share it with my people?"

"Yeah, sure."

Things were mended between us. Then, Saturday morning, I presented myself at the bed-and-breakfast. I wore brown.

Aunt Melanie recited the rules quietly: "Deer lead us back to the early primal teachings. They represent gentle love. And forgiveness. Humans have confiscated their environment, shot them, run them over with cars, hunted them for food. And they forgive us. You have a lot of forgiving to do in your life, Millicent. They are a good choice for you."

I nodded.

"Remember that most magic takes place primarily in the mind, only at a different level of perception. You may not really change your shape into a deer, only think you have. But it makes no difference, as long as you have undergone the transformation inside and believe it has physically occurred."

"Yes," I said.

"Keep in mind that although we are doing this without your brother's permission, he is still the guardian of your earthly existence. We are the guardians and teachers of your magical one. We do this not to flaunt your power, but to make you realize your innate gifts, to fulfill your destiny. We ask you now to reaffirm your understanding of this."

"I do," I said.

We were outside, at the edge of the garden, behind the bushes. I had already danced off my sacred space and was in the center of it.

"The door, the door," Aunt Mercy reminded Aunt Melanie.

"Yes, you must visualize a door," Aunt Melanie said. "On it is engraved the image of the deer. When you are ready, visualize the door opening, and you going through it as a deer. When you are ready to come back—and I advise no more than two hours—you come back through the door, and visualize it closing behind you. Once that happens you will be yourself again."

"Take this new amulet." Aunt Melanie put a string of red

wool around my neck. It had six chestnuts knotted in it.

"Now, dear," she said, "give me your four-leaf clover."

I gave it to her.

"Did you pick this at the hour of Jupiter before sunrise on the first Tuesday of a new moon?" Aunt Melanie asked.

"Yes," I answered.

She put it in a dish at my feet that held four burning candles, mumbled a spell, then reached for a box of salt and threw some over both my shoulders.

Aunt Mercy peeled an apple. The skin came off in one long piece. She mumbled a spell and looped it through the wool around my neck. "Give this to your friends, as an offering."

Then we held hands. "While we do the next spell, you visualize, Millicent," Aunt Melanie instructed.

I breathed deeply and saw myself as a young doe. My aunts stopped mumbling. Now it was my turn.

"I shall go into a fawn," I said, "with joy and respect and such and mickle care for this creature whose shape I beg to take on; and I shall go in the animal spirit's name, aye, and walk among them, and hear their joys and woes, and I'll come home again."

Their hands dropped away. Then I heard my own breathing. In my mind I saw the door with the engraving of the deer on it.

I heard Aunt Melanie's voice, a distance away from me now. "Two hours, dear. You don't need a watch. You'll know."

Then Aunt Mercy: "Remember to come back through the door."

I walked through it. A bird called. The sound was clear and piercing. I heard water rushing in a brook, smelled the herbs in the garden as I'd never smelled them before. Then I smelled Aunt Melanie's still-blooming geraniums and felt a sudden hunger for them.

My aunts were at the back door of the house, waving. I picked up my hand to wave back, but couldn't.

My hand was suddenly a foot!

It had worked! I was a deer!

Or was it only in my own mind? Then I remembered what Aunt Melanie said. It didn't matter.

Chapter
Fifteen

I ran through the fields. I had no time to waste. Oh, I could hear things better. A car out there on the road sounded like a freight train. And what was that other sound?

Music. A kind of symphony that was sad and wonderful all at the same time. But wait, it wasn't music.

It was wind!

I felt it on my face, soft and caressing. It seemed to sparkle in front of me, and I could see grains of sunlight in it. And the music it made was like a chorus. I listened.

"You leave bits of yourself in the air every time you speak. Every word lingers and makes the atmosphere healthy or unhealthy. Learn, little sister, learn, to go with the good air currents in your life, and avoid the harmful ones that surround evil people. And if you find yourself in bad currents, change them with a good word. Go now, go."

I stopped at the narrow road, looked carefully both ways, and went across to the wooded side, down the hill, and over a wooden bridge that crossed a stream.

I felt so free, so strong, as if I could run forever, but I wasn't accustomed to such narrow ankles, and I didn't want to break one of my legs, so I walked.

Half a mile up the road was Mom's house, a short distance from the Beringers'. A small woods of poplar trees separated them. Nobody was home at the Beringers'. There was a football game that afternoon. I went, cautiously, through their place, sniffing, and smelled sadness, rot, evil. I ran to the edge of our property. Mom was near. I knew. I could smell her.

She was sweeping off the patio. I peeked through the bushes and watched her and felt the currents of sadness flowing toward me from her, and, as the wind had advised me earlier, I tried to say some good words for her.

"You will sell your new paintings, Mom," I said. "Don't worry." Mom had sternly forbidden me to use my wish to help her in any way. But I knew, in my bones, that she would sell them.

I'd stepped out from behind the bushes, to intercept the sad currents and turn them away. And then she saw me. I turned and ran down the slope in back of the house to the stream. Looking back, the house looked sturdy and safe, but the woods seemed better to me just then.

Their dimness welcomed me. Underfoot I felt the soft earth, heard it sigh, heard the insects going about their business and nuts falling from the trees, and saw two squirrels arguing over them.

"Why are you two fighting?" I asked. It did not surprise me that they would speak to me.

"This is the way we play, don't you know? We consider play as important as scurrying around and building our nests in the hollows of the trees. Don't you play?"

"Not much anymore," I admitted.

The second squirrel shook its tail. "If you don't balance

out work and play, the work will cause problems. What are those nuts you're wearing?"

"My amulet," I told them.

"You'd better bury them quick," one squirrel said. "Save. Plan for the future."

I thanked them and went on.

A robin darted across my vision and perched on a nearby branch. "I told them, I told them, we should be gone by now. Here it is well into September. What are we doing, hanging around? They're getting spoiled, what with the mild winters. One of these days we're going to get caught in a snowstorm in October. Oh hello, deer. How are you?"

"What's the trouble?" I reached out with my nose.

"Trouble? What could be trouble about trying to get all these flighty friends together for the eight-thirty-five South tomorrow? They leave later every year, no matter what I say."

"Where did you really get your red breast, Robin? I've heard so much about it."

The head cocked. "I pulled a thorn from Christ's head while he hung on the cross, and the blood spilled all over me. I tried to do my part. Couldn't get anybody else to help."

"I've heard the powder-blue color of your eggs represents will, force, and creativity."

"My wife's eggs," he corrected. "But yes, thank you. Well, nice chatting with you. I've got to fly. We've got to be on the eight-thirty-five tomorrow morning."

I went on, laughing.

The woods were alive all around me, with things I'd never been aware of before. Every fallen branch, leaf, stone, and bit of undergrowth stood out as if I'd just painted it with my eyes.

"Well, what's wrong with me, me, me?"

A crow circled my head. "Think you're too good for me, do you? Well, who do you listen to when hunters are near?"

I stopped, eyeing him. "It's just that you're so black, that you disappear into the shadows."

He sat on a large nearby stone. "I used to be white, white as a swan, way back in the times when gods roamed the earth."

"So what happened?"

"I brought some bad news to Apollo one day, and he got so mad he turned me black. But let me tell you, black is beautiful. I'm the smartest bird there is. And where I am, there's magic, you can bet on that."

"But why do you make so much noise?"

"Have to. I symbolize spiritual strength and the magic that's in everybody. Think you can get the people to pay attention to the magic in themselves? You try it."

"Tell me more about yourself." I knelt down next to him.

"Well, we always keep sentinels posted to be on the lookout. We build our nests high in trees so we can see everything. No surprises. We want no surprises. We're the first to raise an alarm when things go wrong."

"But you steal from other birds. I've seen you."

"Well, we need more food than other birds. What's a little thievery between friends? Did you know that when the prophet Elijah went hiding in the wilderness, we fed him?"

"No."

"Don't know much, do you? Before you go, there's something I've got to tell you. We crows are pikers compared to what you humans do. You've had a lot of thievery in this town, haven't you?"

"You know that, too?"

"I not only know, but I've seen 'em do it. I know who it is! I know who it is!" He flew into a tree, shouting it.

"Stop bragging and tell me."

"You know, too. The guy who offered you a ride the other day. And he's got a helper. I know where he's hiding the stuff."

"Where?"

"Your place, your place, your place."

"Our house?"

"I didn't say house. I said place, place, place. Yours, yours, yours. I've said enough. Be careful!" And with that, he flew away.

I ran quickly after him, but he was gone. Instead I came face-to-face with three deer, all females. Would they speak to me? Accept me? I crept forward cautiously. They were eating leaves from the lower part of some trees. "Hello," I said.

They didn't stop chewing, but they looked at me, with beautiful liquid eyes. The first deer spoke in a soft, beautiful voice. "Hello, yourself. Who are you?"

"One of you."

"You wish," the second one said. "You look like one of us, but I don't know." She sniffed. "You're human. What is that, one of your silly Halloween outfits?"

"No, I'm gifted with magic, and I'm practicing shape-shifting. I chose to look like a deer."

"Why?" the first deer asked. "So you could spy on us, and tell the hunters where to look?"

"There's no hunting allowed this close to town anymore," I said. "My brother is chief of police, and he enforces that very strictly."

They nodded solemnly, so I asked their names.

"I'm Meltane," said the first deer. "And this," she pointed her nose to the second, "is Nolthe, and this is Elberne."

"I've very pleased to meet you," I said.

"So," Meltane commented, "you're the little girl who lives in that house with all the delicious flowers? I tried, once, to get the roses, and your mother chased me with a broom."

"Mom loves her roses. Her flowers mean a great deal to her. She's put a lot of labor and time and money into them."

"Money?" Nolthe asked. "What's that? Can you eat it? Can you sniff it? Can you lie down in it on a cold night?"

"No," I admitted. "But you shouldn't eat people's flowers. They plant them in an act of love and they are so beautiful."

Elberne stepped forward. "We get hungry. You humans have taken over all our land. Every day we see more and more of your big machines moving the earth, cutting down trees, pushing us away and leaving us nothing."

"I'm sorry," I said. "I know that's true."

"Few people feed us," Meltane said.

"Aunt Mercy does. Why don't you move back more into the wilderness?"

Meltane answered. "In all our lifetimes we never move more than five miles from where we're born. We have a sense of place."

I sighed. "How 'bout I feed you this winter? I'll put the food back near the stream."

"A salt lick, too?" Meltane pushed.

I promised. "And here." I walked toward them. "My aunt gave me this apple peel and nuts as a peace offering."

Nolthe came over and delicately put her teeth on the apple peel and red wool and pulled both off me. "Thank you." She shared it with the others.

Then she looked at me. "Am I wrong, but do I sometimes

hear you crying at night when I'm standing outside your house?"

"You're not wrong," I said. "Sometimes I cry for my daddy. He left us."

"So?" Meltane asked. "Our fathers leave after a few months. They take no part in raising the young. With us, mothers rule. They can, you know."

"Yes," I said. "I know."

"You've got male protectors around," Nolthe reminded me. "We've seen them."

"One's my brother Dexter. He's my twin. And the other's my older brother Mac, who watches after me and Dexter."

"He's strong and capable," Nolthe said. "He carries a great sadness in him. It has to do with a dead child."

Martha, I thought. But why? Does he think, even though he was only eighteen then, that he was responsible for her?

"But he also carries a lot of caring and love. If he were one of us, he'd have a first-rate set of antlers, and you know they mean heightened perception."

"Thank you all so much. I'm so honored to meet you," I said. "But I've got to go. I'm due back."

"Remember what we told you," Nolthe said.

"And don't forget the salt lick this winter," Elberne called out as I turned away.

"Be gentle with yourself," from Meltane. "And in spite of all that's happened to us as a species, we'll never look at you humans with anything but love in our eyes. Remember that, too."

I ran as fast as I could, the good vibes in the air currents pushing me along like waves. My heart was near to bursting with love and happiness.

Chapter Sixteen

The next day was Mabon, the Autumn Equinox. And Dex's and my birthday.

I woke with a grinding, throbbing headache. At breakfast, when I was still in my robe and pj's, Mom kissed us both. "Presents tonight, when the aunts, Mac, and Maddie come," she said.

Dex kissed me. "Go back to bed," he said. "It's tough, turning fourteen. Mom, if it's okay, I'm gonna hang with the guys for a while. Go over yesterday's game. Do I have to go to church?"

Mom excused him and he left right after breakfast. I went back to bed and Mom leaned over me. "I've called the aunts. They'll be over soon. Aunt Mercy says shape-shifting caused the headache. It's a drain on your psyche. But oh, darling, I'm so proud of you."

"Did you ever do it, Mom?"

"Of course." She looked wistful. "I wanted to be a lion. The females are so good with their cubs. But of course, that was impossible in this country, so I did my second choice. A horse. Horses are clairvoyant, you know."

"I can't remember anything about it. Is that all right?"

"Don't worry. It will come back to you with time."

While we waited for the aunts, Mom told me some good news. "Yesterday I got an acceptance for my illustrations for the children's book."

"Oh, Mom! I'm so happy!"

I hugged her. Then, for a moment, there was a whiff of memory, of me watching her sweep off the patio. But it went as quickly as it came.

The aunts came. Aunt Mercy gave me a powder for my head, and soon I was sitting up in bed and eating breakfast.

Aunt Melanie brought some hyssop and hung it in the corners of my room to clear out the negativity. She agreed that the headache was from shape-shifting. "But aren't you proud of yourself?" she asked. "And now your moment has come. Do you feel up to it? Receiving your Power today?"

I felt better right off. I got up and put on the special white robe they'd brought. Then we had the ceremony.

We sat in a circle on the floor and passed around a bowl of rose petals, each taking one. Then we turned to the person on our left and pressed the petal to her forehead, cheek, and heart, to release the fragrance.

Next, I stood in the middle of them holding a small white candle Aunt Melanie had given me. It was tied with white ribbons. Each of them grasped a ribbon and made a good wish for me.

"I wish you health," Mom said.

Aunt Mercy wished patience. And Melanie, love.

Aunt Melanie stood beside me with a lighted candle. "You are one with nature," she said. "The Power runs deep in you now. May it flow out upon others, making them whole and giving them peace. May you use it with strength, courage and conviction, kindness, virtue, and integrity."

I blew out the candle. They all clapped and kissed me.

Aunt Melanie gave me a new talisman, a red garnet ring. Red is the color of courage. Aunt Mercy gave me a box of small silver disks covered with geometrical diagrams and Hebrew letters. I could lay them out to make a good spell for someone.

Mom gave me a red velvet pouch. In it were waterproof matches, incense, and some oil to rub on my forehead to get rid of disruptive energies.

These were the gifts for my Power.

Did I feel different? No. But I knew that it was all right. It was a spiritual thing.

I dressed and then went downstairs with them. The aunts stayed all day. We made cauldron cookies and covenstead bread, besides getting ready for Dex's and my birthday supper.

Mom made us a special magical coin cake from a recipe that dates back to the days of the Byzantine Empire.

All afternoon we cooked and laughed in the kitchen.

Mac came. Then Maddie. And we had a wonderful supper and for once everyone got along, though Dex was kind of quiet. You could feel the positive energy floating above us as we sat at the table. Dex and I got plenty of presents.

Mac gave each of us a watch. As he fastened mine around my wrist, he looked at me. "It comes off," he said gently. "For gym."

I hugged him. A lot of water ran under the bridge with me and Mac. And it was sometimes too deep to understand. Did he suspect I'd gotten my Power? Nobody had said anything.

But Mac was smart. You couldn't fool him.

Then, just as the cake was brought out, Dad called and spoke to me and Dex in turn. Our presents would be delivered by UPS tomorrow, he said. Then the best part.

He asked to speak to Mom. Dex and I had taken the phone in the great room, and without a word Dex handed the phone to Mom, and we both walked out to leave her alone with her call.

When everybody left and Dex and I were helping clean up the mess, I had a chance to be alone with him.

"You got your Power today, I heard," he said.

"Yeah. Oh, Dex, I'm sorry you didn't get the Gift. I know you'd be great at it. Please don't be mad at me because I have it. I couldn't stand it if you were. And don't make a lot of it with Mac."

"Not mad. Who says I'm mad?"

"Then something's wrong. Tell me. You've been kind of quiet tonight."

He shrugged. "Okay. I'm being followed."

"Followed?"

"Me and Jimmy. Every time we go out in his car. It's happened twice already."

"Who do you think it is?"

"Don't know." But he was hedging now.

"But you have an idea. Am I right?"

"Hey, like with you before, you can't tell Mac, okay?"

"Sure."

"You remember what Maddie once said about Jimmy taking drugs?"

"Yes."

133

"Well, he isn't using. But I think he's selling. And jeez, Millicent, I can't snitch on him. He's been my friend. I mean, he isn't trying to sell to me or anything. Doesn't even talk about it to me. But I think maybe whoever's been following us has something to do with the drugs."

Alarm went through me. "Dex, you gotta be careful!"

"I know. And I am. But I can't break off my friendship with Jimmy now. Any more than you could break off yours with Naomi. He's done so much for me."

I nodded, agreeing. "Just be careful," I cautioned again. "I mean, friendship only goes so far. But you don't want to get in trouble. Or hurt."

"I won't," he said.

I could tell he felt better sharing this with me. Then he asked me a favor.

"In a couple of weeks it'll be Jimmy's eighteenth birthday. Will you come with me to the mall and help get a present?"

I said I would.

He went upstairs then, and I worried about him. He's too decent, I thought. Like Mac.

Magic would have helped Dexter, taught him some things, protected him even, stabilized him.

I decided to do a spell to give him some protection.

September was going by like a shot. On the upside, I'd written two articles for the school paper and gone to two football games. On the downside, I'd flunked a math quiz and gotten in trouble with the principal and gym teacher. I made sure to take my new watch and ring off for gym. What with having my Power and all, I decided to knuckle down and keep a low profile with the magic.

No sense in aggravating Mac.

But I found time in the next week to borrow Mom's *Complete Book of Spells.* I wanted to do a spell of protection for Dexter.

First I looked up the days when a person most needs protection. Saturday, the day of Saturn, a real nice god who ate his young. "A day of destruction, danger, and death," the book said.

Deceit, too, it said. Joseph in the Bible was sold to the Ishmaelites on a Saturday.

There was a medieval protection, but it required you to draw three drops of blood from the person threatening you—one from the teeth, the second from the lungs, the third from the heart's very core.

Not much chance I could do that.

Another gave protection in war and advised using parts of dead opponents as amulets. No good, either.

Still another involved the fresh blood of a young rooster being sprinkled around the house. And, much as Mom would understand, I didn't think she'd appreciate it.

I looked under herbs. Balm of Gilead mended broken hearts. Dill fought off spells. Blood root left on a witch's doorstep reversed any spell she put on you. Nope.

Then I found it. Ten blades of yarrow. Good, I could get that from Aunt Mercy. I'd have to somehow put nine in one of Dex's socks, and throw one away as a tithe to the spirits. Easy enough. I'd get the yarrow from Aunt Mercy tomorrow.

Mac went away that week for a couple of days to a meeting of the county police chiefs. And while the cat was away, the mice played.

There were two more robberies, in town. A 22 caliber Sentinel High Standard pistol was stolen from one house, and a laptop, jewelry, and cellular phones were stolen from another.

On the first Monday in October, I went to school to find Naomi wearing a whole new outfit. New boots, a short leather skirt with a chain belt, and a short expensive silk top that showed her midriff. She also had some gold chains around her neck, clunky designer shoes, and white silk tights that pulled up above her knees but showed her thighs.

"Wow!" I said. "If those things were reported stolen, the authorities would be blaming you."

She tossed her head. "My mom works for her money. And I've been baby- and house-sitting a lot." She sounded defensive.

"Hey, I was only kidding."

I worried through Social Studies and Biology about offending her. Then, come lunchtime, I had more things to worry about.

Chapter Seventeen

A buzz was starting in school about me. I noticed it in my morning classes, but then I told myself I was only imagining things, being still extra sensitive from my shape-shifting experience.

In the lunchroom I knew better. The first one to come up to me was none other than Jimmy Beringer himself.

Now, as anybody who's lived awhile on this planet knows, football stars do not approach lowly freshmen in school. They do not deign to speak to you. You are not even supposed to say hi to them in the hallways.

They have a mythology all their own. In the pecking order, Jimmy was like King Arthur, warrior, hunter of magic boars, killer of giants, witches, and monsters.

"Hey, Millicent," he said. "How's it goin'?"

Everybody in the lunchroom saw the "new girl" daring to talk to the football star.

"Hi, Jimmy. Fine." I gulped.

"We got this important game Saturday night, you know?"

"I know," I said.

"Yeah, well." And I swear, the hunter of magic boars, the

warrior, the killer of monsters, looked shyly at the floor. "Dexter told me about you."

A bell went off in my head. "Oh?"

"Yeah. You and your magic stuff. You know?"

Blood pounded in my ears. I'd kill Dexter! "Oh, that," I said offhandedly, trying to brush it aside.

"Yeah. He said you had this power. And you could, like, make a wish?" He was blushing now. "Well, Saturday night's important in the conference, you know? Centerville is favored. So, do you think maybe you could make a wish for our victory?"

What did he think, this dweeb, that I'd use my wish for a football victory? The nerve! Then I realized that he didn't understand the importance of it. So I handled it the only way I could.

"With you in there playing for us, Jimmy, the team doesn't need my wish," I said. "But I'll have a good thought."

He blushed even more. "Thanks."

I breathed again and went to find a table in the lunchroom, making believe I didn't see the admiring glances of several senior girls. Wait till I tell Aunt Melanie, I thought.

I sat down with Naomi. But soon Liz and Meredith came over. "What did he want?" Liz asked unbelievingly. "Did he ask you out on a date?"

"Not much chance of that," I said.

"Would you go if he did?"

"I'm not allowed to date yet. Mom said not until I'm sixteen." Actually, Mac had said it, and it was a war zone with us. "Fifteen, if I think you're grown up enough," was all he'd say. But I didn't want to get into that with my friends.

Liz and Meredith had to leave, but Naomi stayed. I could

feel the coldness from her. "Didn't I tell you they'd just want to be friends because of your magic?" she asked.

"Yes, you did."

"Don't be afraid to set them straight."

Only she didn't give any advice about how I was supposed to do that. Then Miss Hardcase came over and sat down right across from me.

"Naomi, excuse us, please. I must speak to Millicent alone."

Naomi left.

Would this woman give me no peace? What had I done now? I'd apologized to her about gym, and to Mr. Rudolphi, on Mac's orders. Wasn't that enough?

"Everybody's heard it by now," she said. "That you have been granted some kind of special power, to make a wish and help people."

I chewed the last of my sandwich, which was starting to taste like volcanic ash in my mouth.

"Look," she leaned forward, "I know we haven't been friends. But you understand that I did what I had to do."

"Sure," I said.

"Right now I have some medical problems. Lumps in my neck area. I've been to the doctor, and I don't want this to get around. I haven't told anybody yet. But I'm afraid it's cancer. Could you make a wish for me that it isn't?"

I closed my eyes briefly. Oh God, I thought, is this how it's going to be, then? Every day of my life?

"I only have one wish," I said.

She smiled. "I'm not saying I believe in that stuff or anything. But like I said, I'll try anything right now."

Oh yeah, sure, right. She wouldn't give me the satisfaction

of believing, but hey, make a wish for me. Just in case.

"I'll think about it," I said.

She gave me a funny look, got up, and walked away. Gym was going to be a miserable affair the rest of the year. I just knew it.

It didn't stop there, either. It went on the whole rest of the day. A girl I didn't know, a senior with beautiful blond hair who was running for class president, came up to me in the hall between classes.

"Cathy D'Angelo," she said. "You're Millicent MacCool, the girl with the special power?"

"I suppose so," I said.

"Look, my little sister has problems. She's five, and she can't talk. My mom's taken her to all kinds of doctors already, and nobody's got an answer. She can hear, but she either can't or won't talk. They all said we should just give her time."

She had tears in her eyes. I looked into those gorgeous brown eyes, and I saw Mac at eighteen, maybe wishing he had his Power so he could save Martha.

"I've had a bunch of requests already today," I told her, "and I've only got one wish."

"Oh," she said, "you poor kid. I'm sorry. Well look, you're Catholic, aren't you? Say a prayer for her, then."

And she was gone.

The next one was a girl I vaguely knew, a freshman named Lucy Elkhorn. She usually stayed to herself.

"Could I ask you something, Millicent?"

"Sure."

"I overheard some of the girls whispering before. Is it true you have magic powers?"

I nodded yes, without speaking. I want out of this school, I was thinking. I'm not going to be able to stand this.

"My dad's been out of work since early last summer. He needs a job. Could you use some of that power to get him one?"

"Oh, Lucy."

"It's okay." She started to move away. "I mean, I bet everybody's bothering you. But just in case, think of me."

Miss Bartle, my math teacher, had no requests. All she had to say was that we were going to have a surprise test, then and there, and she hoped we'd studied. Then she passed out the test papers and looked at me.

"No shenanigans, MacCool," she said. "Heard all about you. I find out you're using any magic in here to ace this test, and I'll know it. You hear?"

Everybody giggled. I said yes, and wondered what magic I could possibly pull to ace the test. The only magic I had right then was in knowing that I was going to flunk it.

By the end of the school day I was really wondering if I could turn my Power back in. Reject it. I had to face these people every day, knowing they all needed help. How could I choose which one to give my wish to, if I wanted? It wasn't fair.

By the time I walked across the schoolyard to where my bike was locked, I knew what I was going to do.

Mac was back from the conference, in his office.

"Hi, how was the trip?" I asked.

"Great. How's things at home?"

"Fine."

He gave me a casual sidelong glance. "To what do I owe

the honor of this visit?"

"Mac, I wanna go back to being home-tutored."

He nodded slowly. He thought a minute. He leaned back in his chair. "This wouldn't have anything to do with the fact that you decided to take your Power, would it?"

So he had known. Just hadn't mentioned it. I met his eyes. There was that piercing vision, seeing through me.

I shrugged.

"I've been straight with you, Millicent. And you didn't even have the decency to tell me what your decision was." The voice was low, gentle, but that didn't mean anything.

I felt ashamed. "I felt bad about going against what you asked me to do, Mac."

He nodded. "But you wanted the Power."

"Yeah."

"Well, now you've got it."

I looked down at my hands in my lap. "I'd give it back today, if I could."

He gave a short laugh, threw a pencil on the desk, and put his hands behind his head. "It's gonna get worse before it gets better," he said. "So is it the reason you wanna leave school?"

I shrugged. "You don't know what it's been like, Mac. Everybody knows. And everybody's driving me crazy."

"And how did everybody find out?" He narrowed his eyes. "Dexter?"

I shrugged and looked down. Darn, I shouldn't have come.

"Okay. I'll ask him." He pushed his chair back and put his foot on a lower drawer. "Can't take the heat, huh?"

I told him then about some of the requests. "I can't see

those people every day and have them waiting for me to fix their problems, Mac. I just can't do it."

"Well, you're gonna have to do it. 'Cause I want you in that school. Time to get out in the world and learn how to roll with the punches. You can't be sheltered all your life. Why do you think I won't let you date?"

"To be mean."

"You've been too sheltered, Millicent. You don't even know how to talk to boys."

"I talk to you and Dexter."

"We're not boys. We're your brothers. Anyway, this isn't about dating, so let's not start in on that, okay?"

"Okay, but Mac, you don't know the problems I have now."

"I do know. It's something like winning the lottery. Everybody is happy for you, but they all need money."

That was it! How did he know? Mac didn't need magic, I decided. He had his own methods of divination, his own inner voice.

He spoke slowly. "I was eighteen when Martha died. Fooled around getting my Power. Torn between what Mom believed and what Dad believed. I should have had it already. I could have saved her."

I stared at him. "But you rejected it."

"After she died. What could I do with such Power then? I've never been sorry for a minute. It's a curse, Millicent. Take my word for it."

I looked at him shyly. "It doesn't have to be, if you use it right."

"I've got no authority over this part of your life. Go to people who do."

"Sure."

He leaned forward. "But I'm still gonna give you advice. Use it quick. Get rid of it. And be done with it. And all the attendant magic. Before you meet up with some guy who means a lot to you. You chose it, deal with it. You know right from wrong."

"I feel it's right for me to be home-tutored. Some kids get home-schooled through high school."

"I do not want to hear about leaving school again!" The voice was stern, emphatic.

"But what am I gonna do about all those people who keep coming to me?"

"Listen to them. Sympathize. That helps. In my job they call it sensitivity training. That's all they need. And learn how damned lucky you are. And while you're at it, have some sympathy for your brother. Because he's gonna get hell for blabbing about you all over school."

"Oh, Mac, please don't."

"Don't tell me what to do. You've got enough of your own business to mind."

I was hurt. Tears came to my eyes. Mac saw them but didn't care. And that hurt even more. He'd always been a harbor for me, a final, safe refuge. And now he was turning me away.

"Now get out of here. I'm busy." His eyes were hard.

I got up to leave. I was numb with hurt. Of course he wouldn't let me quit school. I shouldn't have asked.

I shouldn't have come! Somehow I got out of there without bawling and making a fool of myself.

"Now now," Aunt Melanie said, "don't cry. He's right. He

has no control over this part of your life, and he knows it. He's powerless, and it scares him. Men never like being powerless, honey."

I'd ridden there on my bike after leaving Mac's office. "But Aunt, he's never been this way with me before. No matter what I did."

"Well?" She dabbed my eyes with a handkerchief sprinkled with lavender. "You're growing up. That's hard enough for him to take. He's going to fight everything that takes you away from him."

"But my Power doesn't take me away from him."

"It does in the sense that he can't go there. This magic business really makes him crazy. Even I didn't know he was this set against it."

"What am I going to do about school?"

"Come on. I'll show you how to do some spells, to keep people from bothering you. There's one that's on Shakespeare's tombstone that's just wonderful."

She mixed a potion and said it. "'Good friend for Jesus' sake forbare, to dig the dust enclosed here. Blessed be the man that spares these stones, and cursed be he that moves my bones.'

"You see, in those days they dug up corpses and sold them to doctors so they could do autopsies and learn," she said.

I felt better when I left Aunt Melanie's. I always did. When I got home, Mom was so excited. There was a gorgeous bouquet of flowers, just delivered. The card said, "Congratulations and love, from Mac, Maddie, Dex, and Millicent."

"So beautiful," Mom said. "Thank you all."

Mac'd been so mad at me, he forgot to tell me he'd sent

it. Because I knew he had. That was the other side to him, the side he'd turned away from me earlier.

I didn't think things could get any worse for me, but they did.

Chapter Eighteen

"You're confused," Mom said when I told her about school. "The initial joy of receiving your Power has now changed into the realization of the responsibility. And you're a little scared, that's all."

"I'm all right," I said. I didn't tell her about the trouble with Mac. She was in a good mood from selling her paintings and from the flowers Mac sent. Mom deserved some peace and good moods.

"It's normal, given the circumstances. I remember being the same way. So was your sister. Why don't I call her? She'll talk to you."

"No, Mom, don't. I don't need Maddie."

She insisted. And called. "Now, give her a chance," she said, putting down the phone. "She wants to be a worthwhile big sister, just like Mac wants to be a worthwhile big brother. You can't deny her, Millicent. I insist you be nice."

I promised I would be, and Maddie came over after supper. I was in my room doing my homework.

"Ta-da!" She stood there in the doorway, dressed all in black as always, raising both arms to announce herself. In one hand was a plastic cup of coffee from the local deli, in the other a doughnut.

She hadn't even knocked. "Here I am, your big sister to the rescue. Are you overwhelmed? Well, you've come to the right person. I'm overwhelmed all the time."

"You mean you're going to help me with my math?"

"Yeah, right." She kissed me. "Congratulations, honey. I'm glad for you." She sat down on my bed. "Scared, huh?"

"No," I objected. I supposed I should have been glad she was here. We hadn't really spoken since the business with Dennis and the water in the basement.

"Well, look, I can't stay long, but I just wanted to tell you, if it's that much of a drag, having this magic, get rid of it as soon as you can. Mom told me what happened at school. That's what happened with me," she remembered gloomily. "I tell you, it ruined my friendship with lots of people. So I finally used it to get Spencer to date me. Just to be rid of it."

"You mean you really didn't want him to date you?"

"Of course I did! I was crazy about him! And look what I got for it." She sipped her coffee solemnly. "Look, just don't be taken in by the heaviness of all of it," she said. "You're just a kid. You haven't even dated yet. You're not responsible for saving the world. Or anybody but yourself."

"Sure," I said.

"I know we've had fights. But you mean a lot to me. Don't let it mess up your life, is all. And if you think it's about to, use it and be rid of it. That's all I'm saying. Understand?"

"Yeah. Thanks, Maddie." Funny, she should give the same advice as Mac. Then I thought about how both she and Mac had had a tough time of it. Maybe Mac was right—the magic was a curse after all.

We talked for a while, and then Maddie left. I went on with my math. I heard Dex come home and go to his room. Then the phone rang. I picked it up and heard Mom telling Dex it was Mac. For him.

I put it down.

About fifteen minutes later Dex pushed open my door. "Thanks for snitching on me to Mac."

My stomach fell. He looked miserable. He stood there, hands thrust into his pockets. His face was white. Mac, I thought. Mac nailed him. That's what it did to you.

"Dex, I didn't snitch. He asked me how people in school knew about me."

"And you said it was my fault?"

"I didn't say. Mac just figured."

"Yeah, well, you didn't have to go running to him in the first place, did you?"

"What happened?"

"I gotta tell you I'm sorry for blabbing all over school about you, or he's gonna take away my stereo, TV, and computer games for a month. The telephone wires between here and downtown are all burned up."

"I'm sorry, Dex."

"He said I should learn to keep my mouth shut. And keep certain things in the family and not blab them around."

He fell silent for a minute, then said it. "I'm sorry."

"It's okay, Dex."

"You know what it means to catch hell from Mac? No, you don't. He never yells at you! You never get punished, either."

"I do so! Look how he cut off my amulet."

"You call that punished?" He turned to go.

I got up and ran to him. I grabbed his shirt. "Dex, don't be

mad. Jeez, I can't stand it when you're mad at me. Oh, Dex."
I hugged him, but he resisted. He stood there, unyielding.

"Everybody spoils you," he said. "They think 'cause I'm
a boy . . . " He didn't finish his sentence.

"Dex," I said, "Mom was twenty-two when she had Mac
and forty when she had you and me. You know that?"

He shrugged.

"She wanted another boy. Mac was going off to college. So
she had us at forty. It was you she wanted, Dex. I came along
just for the ride."

"That's not true, about you coming along just for the
ride."

"Mom wanted a boy," I said. "She wanted you."

I watched him go back across the hall to his own room.
"I've thought of a gift you can get Jimmy for his birthday," I
said. "How about a Dallas Cowboys sweatshirt? I'll go with
you to the mall to get it."

"Sure," he said.

Chapter
Nineteen

Things quieted down somewhat. Aunt Melanie's spell must have worked, because I wasn't bothered in school anymore. At least that's what I thought, until Dex told me what he'd done one day when we were carving pumpkins for the front of the house.

"I got word around that you're just like everybody else, that I was spinning a story just to make your first weeks in a real school rough," Dex said. "Sort of like an initiation."

I couldn't believe it. "You did that for me?"

"Sure. I messed things up for you, didn't I? And hey, don't forget, I can lie."

"I wish I could, Dex. You don't know how much."

There was one spell I did ask Aunt Melanie to do for me, though, the one for Cathy D'Angelo's little sister.

I watched as she thumbed through the worn pages of her spell book. It took a while. We were in her private parlor, candles lighted all around.

"This child is fairy struck," she finally decided.

I liked the sound of it. It fit. "What must we do?"

"Such children often pine away. We need the juice of

twelve leaves of foxglove. Let's go into Aunt Mercy's herb closet."

There we found the foxglove. Then Aunt Melanie created her circle, the boundary between us and the physical world. She gave me a piece of parchment and I wrote down, with a quill pen, my petition for Cathy's little sister. While I did this she chanted some prayers and burned some cobs of corn in a bowl as an offering. "Raise your hands. Let the energy go," she directed.

I did so. She gave me the juice of the foxglove. "Tell Cathy to mix it with her sister's orange juice. And here. Take these rowan branches and tell her to place them above the child's bed."

Cathy's eyes opened wide when I gave her the stuff in school. "But everybody is now saying it was all a joke about you," she said.

I put my finger to my lips. "Only for you. I know you can keep a secret," I said. "And anyway, my aunt Melanie did the spell, not me. And she's experienced."

I helped Mom finish decorating her houses. Dex and I planned our Halloween costumes. We were going to help Mom at the haunted house on Halloween. I would be Morgan Le Fay, King Arthur's half sister. Dex was going to be King Arthur. Aunt Melanie and Mom were working on our costumes. I did a lot of sewing at night, watching TV.

It was the third weekend in October, time for the fall freshman dance. No dates. Boys and girls just mixed. "I dread it, Dex," I said. "I heard that the popular girls are always asked to dance and the others stand there sucking their thumbs and watching."

"No sweat," Dex said. "You're so pretty, you'll be asked, don't worry."

He sounded like Mac.

Costumes weren't worn at this dance because they were saved for the next weekend. Maddie said she'd help me shop for a dress.

"I want a long skirt," I told Mom, "with a slit up the side. And a new sweater."

I have to say one thing about my sister, she knows clothes. The skirt was a silvery blue, the sweater black, and Mom gave me her long pearls to wear.

The boys could wear jeans, but they had to wear collared shirts, ties, and jackets.

Except for the fact that everybody looked at me because I walked in with Dexter, and that Ryan Beaumont, Dex's friend, asked me to dance one of the first dances, the whole thing was terrible.

First off, either the gym was too cold or I was too nervous. Second, the music was so loud and disjointed that it brought out all the negative energy. I couldn't find my middle path of equilibrium so my mind and body could work in unison.

Even in dancing this is important.

Third, the boys I went to school with every day all strutted around trying to be grown-up in jackets and ties, but anybody could see they weren't in harmony with nature and their physical and spiritual worlds were not aligned.

Why do they make freshman girls hang out with freshman boys? I wondered. Boys at that age have so much more growing to do. I doubt even a *senior* would have his physical and spiritual worlds aligned yet, much less a freshman.

Dex asked me to dance once, too. "You okay?" he asked.

"All the guys I danced with had no personal power," I said.

"C'mon, Millicent. You looked like you were having fun."

"Thanks for having Ryan dance with me."

"I had nothing to do with it."

I looked up at him. It was one of the few slow dances, so I could look into his eyes, see if he was lying.

He wasn't.

"He thinks you're pretty," Dex told me.

I wished he hadn't told me that, because when Ryan asked me for another dance, I had to take some slow, relaxing breaths. And I found my middle path of equilibrium for a time, at least. He was almost as handsome as Dexter, only he had reddish hair. We got some punch together and I found myself chatting away with him.

Afterward I thought, I gotta remember to tell Mac that it's not the way you talk to boys that matters. It's the way they talk to you.

Three-quarters of the way through the dance, I escaped to the girls' room.

Naomi was there, and in two minutes I wished I hadn't come in.

"We're the only two wearing long skirts," she said.

True. Hers was orange and red, colors that signified outrageous behavior.

"So you're off the hook with the magic, I heard," she said. "Dex got word around that it was all a joke."

"Yeah. I hope they believe him."

"Some do. But from what I hear, your family's reputation precedes you. I think you'll still be getting some requests."

I sensed something coming.

"Would you still do something, if somebody worthwhile asked you?"

Why did I want to run out of there? More to the point, why did I stay?

"I need you to help me, Millicent." She looked tearful.

"What's wrong?"

"My dad. You know all the robberies in town?"

"I don't think I want to hear this, Naomi." I turned to walk away, but she grabbed my arm. "Are you a friend or aren't you?" she demanded.

I sighed and stood still.

"My dad's been robbing the houses."

Naomi told stories sometimes. "Your dad isn't even around, Naomi. Nobody's seen him."

She gave a short, bitter laugh. "That's how much you know. You and that clever brother of yours. My dad's been in town for weeks now. And he's right under everybody's noses." She smiled. "He changed the color of his hair and wears a mustache. And he's been stealing, hitting all the houses. You know where he's hiding the stuff?"

"Don't tell me any more, or I'll have to tell Mac."

"You can't." Again the hand on my arm, restraining me. "Remember we made a blood promise to be friends forever? Well, what do you think that means? You break the promise and you lose your Gift. At least that's the way I understand it."

I stood, stricken.

"In your secret place." She gave a small smile of triumph. "When's the last time you were there?"

"I haven't been lately. I've been too busy."

"Well, I figured you'd be going there Halloween, since it's

155

got such a special meaning to you. So I had to tell you. Besides, I need your help, Millicent. Please!"

Then she had a brainstorm and checked all the booths to make sure nobody was there. We were alone.

"My dad's luck isn't going to hold out forever," she said. "Sooner or later he's going to get discovered. I keep telling him he has enough loot."

"You've seen it?" I asked.

"Of course. I helped him get some of it. Why do you think I'm wearing a long dress tonight?" She turned and picked up the hem. The back of her legs had red welts. "My dad's signature," she said.

I felt sick. "He beats you to make you help him steal? You break into houses? That's child abuse. Why don't you tell somebody?"

She raised her eyes to the ceiling. "Oh, Millicent, you live in such a nice safe little world. It doesn't work that way for some people. He's my dad. How much do you love your dad?"

"Not enough to help him steal."

"No. Because he's rich. But suppose he wasn't? Suppose he just got out of prison and needed a new start? And promised you this was just temporary, this stealing, and when he got enough he was going to leave and take you with him?"

"Naomi, I don't want to hear any more about this."

"You can't leave." She grabbed my skirt, stopping me. "You think you're so special, with your rich dad who flies in on planes, your police chief brother, and your mom in that big house."

"I never said I was special."

"Well, you act it. But you're no more special than I am.

And you're going to help me now, because you swore to be friends forever."

I closed my eyes and leaned against a sink. I felt sick to my stomach, the way you do when you're trapped. "What do you want, Naomi?"

"Use your wish to help me. Us. My family. I need my dad to stop stealing, to take his stuff and leave. And take me with him." Her tone was softer now. "Please, Millicent. I'm afraid he's going to get caught again. I'm afraid I am. You don't think I want to go to jail, do you?"

"I don't think I can use my Gift to help somebody make a moral decision," I said. "We all have free will. I'm not that powerful, Naomi."

"You just don't want to!" she said angrily.

I faced her. "You were the one, all along, who warned me that kids who wanted to be friends with me would only want what I could do for them."

"That's right," she said. "Somebody had to warn you."

"I thought our friendship was special. Because you never asked me for anything."

"Look, I never intended to."

I turned away. "Don't lie on top of it all, Naomi. You were planning to all the time."

"Think whatever you want," she said. "You've still got to help me, or break our blood promise."

I had to get control of myself. I had to think. "I need time," I said. "And if I don't go back out there now, Dex and Ryan will wonder what happened to me. Let's go back out and pretend everything is okay, Naomi."

"And then what?"

"I need a couple of days, please. Give me two days, and

I'll help you. I promise."

She grinned, triumphant. And I hated her right then. I didn't care, either, if hate was a negative emotion, a waste of time, if it would cause me trouble on the astral plane. I had to live in the here and now, and I knew I was trapped.

Chapter
Twenty

I'll get to it, I told myself over the next couple of days. I'll get to the problem with Naomi by Friday.

But I was so depressed because she'd turned on me. My one true friend! Had she been keeping me as a friend as insurance all along?

I didn't tell anybody, not even Aunt Melanie. I couldn't bring myself to tell anybody how I'd been taken.

I used the oil Mom had given me to banish disruptive energies. I rubbed it so much on my forehead that it hurt. It didn't help. I wasn't practiced enough yet, I told myself. But I knew what the trouble was.

I had refused acceptance. I had refused to see what I was, with all my strengths and weaknesses. I had thought this Power would change everything.

I had to move into what I feared, facing my life in its entirety. And I'd made Naomi part of that entirety, and now I had to deal with it. On my own. Asking nobody.

I knew that I had to face up to my own behavior and decisions. That, in itself, was Power, Aunt Melanie had taught me. Of course, when I did, I might discover that all my difficulties were only the result of my own stupidities and inner turmoil. But at least I'd know, and that, too, was Power.

I set it all aside for the moment and went to the mall with Dexter to get the sweatshirt for Jimmy's birthday.

Then all of a sudden everything changed.

Mom invited Mac over for supper the Wednesday before Halloween so they could talk about how much security she needed at the haunted house. Dex was talking about Jimmy's party on Friday night, because Mom was sending a cake.

"I can't believe Jimmy is growing up so," Mom said. "I've known him since he was a baby."

"Eighteen," Mac said. If he was still angry with me and Dex, he didn't act it. Mac knew what his part was in our lives, and he played it well all the time. No inner turmoil for him.

Dex looked up. "How do you know?"

Mac shrugged. "He used to come over when I played with you kids when you were little, remember?"

There it was again. More symbolism, more signs that I didn't pick up on. I was so nailed to the ground with my own problems.

I didn't even pick up on it the next night when we were at supper and Mac called and asked for me.

"Take the phone in the other room," he directed.

My heart fell inside me. He'd found out about Naomi's father. What would I say to him?

"Millicent, listen to me. I need a favor." His voice was low, serious.

"Sure." I was glad to be asked, anxious to make things up to him.

"Has Dexter spoken about going with Beringer to the

party tomorrow night?"

I breathed a sigh of relief. It wasn't about any robberies. "Well, sure," I said.

"You gotta keep him from going, Millicent."

"Me? You're not gonna let him go to the party and you want me to tell him?"

"He can go to the party, but not with Beringer."

"Why?"

"I can't tell you. But I need this favor from you. Bad. You have lots of influence with Dexter. He'll do just about anything for you. Think up something you need for him to do that'll make him late."

"Mac, what's going on?"

"I can't tell you."

"Oh, great. But I'm supposed to—"

"Yes, you are," he interrupted, his voice hard. "I didn't want to ask you. I know we haven't been getting on. If I could think of another way, I would. But I can't."

"I'll try," I said hesitantly.

"Good girl." The tone changed now, full of affection, warm. "You help me with this and I owe you one, honey."

"Okay, Mac," I said. That was money in the bank, having Mac owe you. And I hoped he'd remember that when he found out I knew about Naomi and the robberies.

Something was going on. But what? Then I knew. It was a no-brainer. Drugs at Jimmy Beringer's party. There would be a raid and it would be before Dexter got there. One minute I thought I had it figured out, the next I didn't. If there was going to be a drug raid, Mac could just forbid Dexter to go. Dex would raise hell, but he'd have to listen.

Damn, I was annoyed. Why was I always the one to help

everybody? How many messes was I expected to straighten out, anyway? And who was helping me?

I thought about it for a day. I'd ask Mom's help, have her be late with the cake she was making for Dex to bring to the party. Then I decided no, I better keep Mom out of it. If Mac had wanted her involved, he would have involved her.

So I beat myself up trying to figure something out. Then Friday in school, Naomi came up to me when I was at my locker.

"Have you thought about helping me?" she asked.

And then I knew what I was going to do. About Dexter, not Naomi. One problem at a time, I told myself.

"Yes," I said to her. "Yes. I'll call you later tonight, Naomi, I promise."

"Dex, I got a problem. I need help."

Sure, I knew I had to handle my problem myself, and ask nobody. But Dex was different. He was my twin. There was a karma between us.

He looked up from the desk in his room. It was Friday, after school.

"What?"

"I need to go to the old half-finished house. Tonight. And I don't want to go alone. I need you with me."

"You ought to stay away from that place, Millicent. This time of year there's likely to be raccoons or squirrels in there. Maybe even snakes. Raccoons could be rabid."

"You sound like Mac."

"Well, it's catching. Anyway, I've got Beringer's party!"

"I know, Dex. But you could be a little late, couldn't you? This is important."

He looked at his watch. "What the hell, Millicent? It's already six. I got all this math, and Jimmy's picking me up at eight."

"If you knew why I have to go, you'd come, Dex," I said.

He sighed. "Okay, tell me."

So I told him. I told him about Naomi and her father stealing and the loot being at the old half-finished house. And how I had to go there and make sure she was telling the truth before I said anything to Mac.

"Her old man's been doing the robberies?"

"Yes."

He shook his head. "And she's been helping. Your friend? Jeez, Millicent." He thought for a moment. "Tonight?" he said. "You gotta go there tonight? Why tonight?"

"A couple of reasons. Kids might go there tomorrow on Halloween and find the stuff. And it's my place."

"And so what are we gonna do after we get there?"

"After I see for sure that the loot is there, I'll probably tell Mac. But I wanna see it first, Dex."

He scowled. "I thought you and Naomi made a blood promise to be friends forever?"

Dexter was too smart. I had to be careful, or I'd lose him now. "I thought maybe you could help me figure that out, too." If he was truly like Mac, he'd like his ego appealed to.

"Jeez," he said again. He shoved his homework aside and reached for his windbreaker. "Okay, come on. Wait, I'll call Jimmy and tell him to go on without me, that I'll be a little late."

I ran across the hall to get my own jacket and a flashlight.

We took our bicycles, telling Mom we'd be right back. It was getting dark when we got there, the chilled dark of an

October night, when you truly realize summer is over and soon the world is going to turn very cold.

"Well, we're here," Dex said.

We left our bikes and went up the path to the house, which stared down at us, blank-eyed. The skeleton of wood framing had been covered with plywood before the building stopped. The roof was on but not shingled. I never could go there without feeling all that positive energy left there by my father.

We went over the doorstep. Dex shone the flashlight around the rooms on the ground floor.

Our footsteps echoed amidst the gathering of old leaves on the plywood flooring as we walked through. Then we saw it, a bunch of stuff in the corner of what I think was supposed to be the living room. A bunch of stuff covered by an old canvas tarp.

"There's the loot," Dex said.

"Should we look?" I asked.

"Guess that's what we came for, isn't it?"

I wasn't sure anymore, what I'd come for. I held the light while Dex removed the canvas, uncovering the stolen property.

There were bags, all kinds of bags, from the local stores. Plastic, paper. In some was clothing, new, with the tags still on. Girls' and women's clothing, pants, blouses, sweaters.

"Looks like it's for Naomi. Or her mom," I said.

"He shoplifted, too, apparently," Dex said.

In other bags was the stuff that had been stolen from local houses. We found the silverware that belonged to Mrs. Agren, still in its own case. A whole stereo was there, two TVs, some women's jewelry, a box of some kind of plates, and a whole mess of other things. Things from houses right in Glen Laurel, things that were meaningful to people.

"Wow!" Dex said. "No, don't touch anything, Millicent. Fingerprints. This is a crime scene." He covered everything with the canvas. "I can't believe your friend helped her father steal this stuff."

"Her father beats her, Dex, to make her help him."

He gave a low whistle. "Boy, and we think we have it bad."

"Yeah, her life really sucks."

"We gotta tell Mac."

"We can't," I said.

"What? What do you mean, we can't?" Dexter's voice cracked.

"I mean I can't. You said it. I can't break my promise."

He looked at me and sighed. "Oh, yeah. Well, I'll tell him, then. That won't hurt your promise to Naomi, will it?"

I shrugged. "I just wonder sometimes, Dex, about this not lying business with me. Am I supposed to keep a promise to somebody who's done wrong? Is that the way it works?"

"Don't ask me how it works," he said. "Just come on and let's get out of here. I'll tell Mac first thing in the morning."

I took a longing look back at the house when we left. I'd shared my secret place with Naomi. Nobody else. And she'd done this. I felt violated.

Chapter
Twenty-One

How could people appear to be one thing all along and then turn out to be something else?

Talk about shape-shifting. Two people did some heavy duty shape-shifting on me that week. Two people at the opposite ends of the food chain: Naomi and Mac.

Mom had taken Dexter to the party and was meeting friends at the haunted house afterward. Aunt Melanie was involved in some kind of Halloween preparations for the bed-and-breakfast. Aunt Mercy was at the hospital.

I was doing my reading on my bed and must have fallen asleep. The sound of the car in the drive and the car lights in my window woke me. I had a terrible feeling something was wrong. Something more than just the fact that I'd gone to sleep struggling between a couple of realities.

"Millicent, Millicent?" Mom was calling me from downstairs. I went out into the hall, then down onto the landing. She was putting lights on in the great room. I looked down at her.

"Oh, honey," she said. "Come on down and make me some hot chocolate. You'll never guess what's happened."

Right about then I saw Dexter. He came through the great room, his shoulders hunched forward in his windbreaker, his baseball cap on backward and tufts of hair sticking up out of it. His hands were thrust into his jeans pockets, and he didn't look at me as he came up the stairs.

"Darling, come down and talk to me." Mom was talking to Dex. "Come on, please."

He whirled around and stood next to me on the landing, looking down at her. "What's to talk about? He did it, didn't he? You'll just defend him. You always do!"

Then he looked at me. "There's no way out with Mac," he said. "There never is."

"There wasn't a way out for your brother, no," Mom said.

I heard tears in Dexter's voice. "He didn't have to do it this way! I'm never talking to him again. I'm gonna call Dad tomorrow and go and live with him."

Fear went through me. "What happened?" I asked. For a minute I thought I was going crazy. Was I still sleeping? Was this a nightmare? It had to be. No matter what differences Dex and I had with Mac, we'd never threatened this.

"He had Jimmy arrested tonight. On the way to the party."

"Arrested? Jimmy?" I stared at him.

"Yeah. Turns out they're the ones who've been following us these past few weeks. The cops. Just waiting for Jimmy's eighteenth birthday. So he can be tried as an adult for dealing."

Then he ran up the stairs and into his room, slamming the door.

I looked down at Mom. "Is it true?" I asked.

"Yes," she said. "Apparently, Mac felt this was the way to

do it. There was turmoil at the party. Dex asked me to take him to the station. We saw Mac for just a minute. He's pretty sure Jimmy was the one who sold drugs to JoLynn Eustis before she died."

"Oh, God," I said. That was the reason Mac had wanted me to make Dexter late for the party. So he wouldn't be in the car with Jimmy when the arrest was made.

"All he'd get as a juvenile was a slap on the wrist," Mom was saying.

I'd been a part of his plan. And it had worked.

"I want Dad's number, Mom. I mean it," Dex said.

We were in the great room in front of a fire about twenty minutes later. Mom had convinced Dexter to come down. None of us could refuse her anything.

"I don't have it, darling, and that's the truth."

"Why doesn't Dad give it to you?"

"I don't want it. I might be tempted to call if I wanted something, and I've been trying to be independent, Dexter. You'll have to ask Mac."

I'd made hot chocolate and some sandwiches. Dex was hungry and he ate without realizing it. He wiped his mouth with his hand. "Okay. I will."

Mom set down the pot of hot chocolate. "I wouldn't ask to go and live with your father if I were you."

"Why not?" He glared at her.

"Well, first," Mom sighed and smiled, her eyes getting all crinkly, her sweet rosebud of a mouth sad, "you're likely to be hurt. He likes things the way they are now. And if you must know it, Dexter, so do I. Think about what you're saying, honey. You'd be moving around constantly. No steady school or friends, no more football. You'd leave here? Your home? Your sister? Me?"

"I'd still see you, Mom. And Millicent could come, too."

It was all too much for me. I was starting to get a headache. I said nothing.

"I couldn't stand to lose you two," Mom said. "You know, when your brother came home to be police chief in this town, it saved our family. As well as him. There are things you don't know, Dexter."

"Well then, why don't you tell me? Why do you and Mac always think Millicent and I have to be protected? We have to live with the results of all this stuff, Mom. It isn't fair."

Dexter was right, but still I said nothing. He seemed so mature all of a sudden, so grown up. I envied him.

"I mean, I only found out a little while ago about how Martha really died," he went on. "And Millicent found out not long before that. This stuff is garbage, Mom, all these big holy secrets in this family."

Mom had tears in her eyes. "Oh, my baby, you're growing up."

Dexter was embarrassed. "Jeez, Mom, what do you think?"

She took out a handkerchief and blew her nose. Then Dexter was more embarrassed. "C'mon, Mom, don't cry."

"It's not sadness, darling. It's what a mother does when she realizes one of her children is getting wiser than she is. So then, all right. I'll tell you. When your brother was in that firefight in the FBI, a little girl was killed."

For an instant I heard Nolthe's voice. "He carries a great sadness in him. It has to do with a dead child." And I understood.

169

"They had children in the house," Mom was saying, "besides a cache of weapons. They had whole families. A man came out holding a child in front of him, waving a gun. Mac knew he could get off a shot without killing the little girl, but his friend said he wanted to take it. Mac let him. The man shoved the little girl out to take the bullet. Then the man fired at Mac's friend and killed him. Mac blames himself for the little girl's death."

"But that's dumb," Dex said.

"Tell your brother that. Tell him what his superiors told him, that hostage situations often go wrong."

Neither Dex nor I said anything.

"Right about then your dad and I were breaking up," Mom went on. "Your father wanted to take you and Millicent with him. It would have killed me, honey. My twins, my babies. And Mac knew it. So when the police chief's job opened up here in town, he went for it. And of course, they loved him. He grew up here. He had all the FBI training. And I loved it because he offered to bring you and Millicent up if your dad left you both with me. Dad agreed and had papers drawn up that Mac was to be your legal guardian."

Dex put his hand over mine on the couch.

Mom cleared her throat. "He was doing it for me, yes. And for you children. But also for himself. I think he needed to make up for the death of that child. And I think it's helped him and is still helping him. It benefited everybody. Don't you see? Your father would have gotten custody after what happened with Martha." She gave a short laugh. "I'm the first to admit it. I was an unfit mother."

"So why does he act like Mac the Knife sometimes, then?" Dex asked.

Mom smiled. "He isn't perfect. He has his weaknesses. Everything with him is black or white. There are no gray areas in between. He gives no quarter. His work makes him this way. So you must remember this when dealing with him."

Dex bowed his head. "He betrayed me," he said.

"Jimmy betrayed everybody," Mom said, "his school, his coach, his mom, and the community."

"I'm talking about Mac. A juvenile arrest would have done it! Now his life is ruined!"

"Jimmy knew that when he started," Mom said. She was so adamant about it, so down-to-earth. It was beyond protecting Mac now. It was the way she got when her family unit was threatened.

"Well, I still want to go live with Dad for a while," Dexter said. "It isn't normal, this way, having my brother bossing me around."

Mom smiled. "Do you know that with the Cherokee Indians, and some other tribes, clan membership passed through the mothers to the children? And responsibility for the younger members fell either to the mother's brother or the children's older brother?"

"Are you telling me we're part Cherokee now, too?" Dex asked.

"No. But the Indians are all very mystical. And so is this family. It seems right the way things are now, is all, considering the things that passed down from me to my children."

"I didn't get any of it," Dex reminded her.

"Maybe you didn't get the Power, but you have other qualities that come directly from me. But go ahead, tell your brother. He should know how you feel. Now I'm tired. I'm going to lock up and go to bed."

I helped her bring everything back into the kitchen. "Mom, you can't let Dex go," I whispered.

"Darling, I wouldn't hold on to him, if it's what he wants."

"Won't Mac?"

"I don't know. But more than anybody Mac knows there's no holding on to anybody if they don't want to be held on to," she said. "Remember, he's been divorced. And it wasn't anything he wanted."

She went up to bed. I went back into the great room. "Dex, wouldn't living with Dad be kind of cutting off your nose to spite your face? Like Mom says, you have everything here."

"Would you come if Dad said yes?"

"I couldn't leave Mom, Dex. I just couldn't do that."

"If it means so much to Mac, raising us, then this is a way to get back at him. Let him know he's failed."

"You really think he's failed?"

"None of the kids I hang with are gonna even talk to me anymore, Millicent. On account of what *my* brother did."

For a moment we just both watched the dying fire. "Maybe they'll blame Jimmy," I said finally. "Don't you think that's where the blame belongs?"

"You sticking up for Mac?" he asked. "I don't see you telling him about the stolen stuff in the house. If you think he's so wonderful, you tell him about it tomorrow, then."

"I can't, Dex. You know I can't."

"Well, you better get your friend and her father to get their stuff out of that old house by tomorrow, Millicent. Tell her I give her till tomorrow night. Or I'm gonna tell Mac."

I stared at his handsome profile in the flickering firelight.

"You were supposed to tell Mac tomorrow morning, Dex," I reminded him.

"To hell with him. I hate his guts right now. Just tell her, will you? And let that be the end of it."

"Sure, Dex," I said.

Chapter
Twenty-Two

I called Mac in the privacy of my room. It was late, but he always liked to watch the eleven o'clock news. He called the murders, rapes, fires bedtime stories.

I knew we'd been at odds, knew I still had to move into what I feared with Naomi, but not yet. Not tonight.

Tonight I needed Mac's silences while he considered what I had to say. And the gentle, hesitant tones when he responded. Tonight I needed the pitch of his voice, even the gruffness, to make me know the sky wasn't going to fall this night while I slept.

"Mac, it's me."

"What's up?"

"I think Dex is going to ask you if he can go and live with Dad."

Silence. Then, "Oh?"

"I just thought you might like to know ahead of time."

"Oh, yeah? He said that, did he?"

"He's pissed at you, Mac. Big-time."

"I don't like that language, honey."

"Well, it's the only word I can think of. He's really sore

because of what you did to Jimmy."

"Is Dex telling me how to do my work?"

"No."

"Are you?"

"No, only I wish you hadn't involved me."

"I involved you so as not to involve Dexter."

"I know, Mac."

"I want to thank you for your help, while we're on the subject. I really appreciate what you did."

"Mac, please don't let Dex go. You're not gonna let him go, are you?"

"He wants to go, let him come and ask me."

"I don't think he really wants to. I think he just wants to hurt you. He hates you right now."

"I don't blame him. I hate myself."

"He just wants to make you think you failed with us."

A longer silence now. Then: "He thinks I failed, is that it?"

"Oh, Mac, he's just sore is all."

"How 'bout you? What do you think?"

"Well . . . " I struggled for a moment. "I get awful mad at you sometimes, but no, not that."

"Hmmm. Well look, like I said, let him come and ask. We'll work it out."

"It would kill Mom if he left, Mac."

"I said we'd work it out. But thanks for warning me. I appreciate it. I owe you two now."

"Mac, I'm not sucking up. I'm doing this for Dexter."

"I don't like that word, either. But I know you don't do that. And you are helping Dexter."

I hung up the phone. More money in the bank, I thought. And somehow I had the feeling I'd need it.

Next morning was Saturday, Halloween. I was up before Dex and Mom. I went into the kitchen and put on a pot of coffee, took Sweetie Pie for a walk, and brought in the newspaper. Then I had some coffee and toast, dressed warm, because the morning was overcast and chilled, left a note for Mom, got on my bike, and made for Naomi's house.

It was neat riding through my neighborhood before most people were up. It was still misty. Crows scolded me from treetops, and I tried to figure out what they were saying but couldn't.

The stuffed witches on people's benches, the ghosts hanging from tree limbs, all waved to me. I passed three houses that I'd helped Mom decorate, then headed out of our part of town.

I knew Mac had forbidden me to go to Naomi's house, and I hadn't been there since midsummer. But this was different.

I was facing up to my own behavior and decisions. I was getting my own Power.

In about half an hour I reached Naomi's house on the other end of town. Here, there were old cars and abandoned refrigerators in the yards. The Town Council had been trying, for years, to get some people to clean the stuff up.

But I thought there were possibilities in this kind of neighborhood. The junk in the yards was like some kind of Americana nobody had recognized yet. Someday they'd be preserving it, auctioning it off as antiques. One guy even had a life-size brown plastic horse in front. Next to it was a plastic white arbor covered with fake roses.

As I pulled into the yard, I saw Mrs. Carlson come out of the side door and get into her car. She waved at me, cigarette in hand. Likely she was going to open the shop.

She was dressed in a costume. I think she was supposed to be a witch. Then I remembered how Maddie said they all dressed up in the shop on Halloween.

I stared at her as if I was seeing some change in the ectoplasm, some real shape-shifting here. How could she be so nice in the beauty salon and allow her husband to beat her daughter?

Naomi opened the door, still in her pj's. She invited me in. "You're gonna do it?" There was an expectant look in her eyes. "You're gonna use your wish to help me? And I can watch. Is that why you're here?"

As a test for myself, I tried some positive visualization, to see her as my old friend. But I couldn't. I felt only revulsion at the way she had betrayed me. And I saw her now as if I'd just gotten laser surgery on my eyes, like one of Mom's friends did.

"Naomi, I don't think my wish is supposed to be used that way."

She reached for a pack of cigarettes. The kitchen was cold, cluttered. There were dirty dishes in the sink. Mom would never let me or Dex leave dirty dishes in the sink, and we always griped about that.

But then Mom would never let anybody beat us, either.

"You don't want to help me."

"I can't. The wish is supposed to be used for the good of mankind." Wow, that didn't come out right. It sounded conceited and lofty. I'd hate me at that moment if I were her.

She did. "Yeah, well, look around you," she said. "Welcome to mankind." She'd lighted the cigarette and was puffing smoke at me.

I drew in my breath. I'd come to the end of the friendship. I was angry one minute, sad the next. Then I thought, Damn, nobody's gonna to do this to me! And then and there I slammed the door on the friendship.

"I know you were friends with me when nobody else from school was, Naomi," I said firmly. "But you were the only one ever invited to my secret place. And what did you do? You let your father put his stolen stuff in it. You defiled it."

"Don't give me that mystic crap."

"You said all the kids were going to be friends with me just to ask me to do them a favor with my magic. And you were right. Part of the time, I think."

"Most of the time."

"Okay, I'll even give you that. But there were real friendships I turned down, because of you. That was all okay while we were friends. But no more. Because you did what you said they'd all do. And so I can't be pushed into this."

"So you're not gonna do it, then." Her voice was flat. Nothing I'd said mattered. Only that I wasn't going to help her.

I finished. "I don't think you have any right to involve me. And you should know, too, that my brother Dex knows about it and he said if you and your dad don't move the stuff by tonight he's going to tell Mac."

She smiled, a secret smile. "I know Dex, Millicent. And I know what happened last night with Beringer. Half the town knows by now. And somehow I don't think Dex is gonna run to his brother with this today."

I raised my chin. "Then I'll tell him."

"You can't, or you'll lose your Power," she answered. "By breaking a blood promise."

"Sometimes right is still right and wrong is still wrong.

And some things are worth sacrificing for," I told her.

More lofty garbage. Why did everything I said come out wrong? So corny. But I meant it. Every word.

"You're not willing to use your Power to help me. But you're willing to lose it by telling on me?"

"Don't make it sound like that," I said.

"But that's what it is."

I moved to the door. I had to get out. There was a line drawn on the old linoleum of the kitchen, like a river of blood between us. You couldn't find anything this bad in Celtic mythology. "Move the stuff by tonight," I said. "I'm going to come and make sure you do."

"Don't." She put out the hand with the cigarette in it. "My dad doesn't know I told you. If you come, he's likely to do something bad. Maybe even hurt you."

"I'll be there," I told her. "As a deer. You'll know me because I'll have a piece of red wool around my neck." I don't know where I got that from. It just came to me. And it seemed right. I put my hand on the doorknob.

I saw her gray-blue eyes widen. "You're lying."

"I can't lie, Naomi. Remember? Either your dad gets that stuff out of there tonight and nobody is the wiser, or tomorrow morning he'll be arrested. Look for me tonight." I went out the door and got on my bike.

She came out and stood there. "I don't care if you come as a deer or as the skunk you are. My dad'll hurt you."

I laughed and rode out of the driveway, wishing I felt as brave as I was acting.

Chapter
Twenty-Three

I went home. There was a note from Mom on the kitchen
table. She'd run over to the haunted house to check on
some last-minute details. Dex was out.

I cleaned my room. I felt the need to be grounded in
everyday chores. I had to keep myself busy, because I wanted,
more than anything, to run over to the bed-and-breakfast and
tell the aunts what I was planning for that evening. And get
their blessing and advice.

But then they might disapprove, even forbid me. And I
couldn't chance it.

Besides, I was facing up to my own behavior. And I had to
do that on my own.

What if Naomi and her father didn't remove the stolen
items from the house tonight?

Then tomorrow I'd go to Mac and confess everything to
him and take my lumps.

It could be the end of me and Mac when he found out I'd
kept this from him. Maybe I'd be the one who'd have to go
and live with Dad. Well, tomorrow was November first, Day
of the Dead. I'd be right in line with things.

* * *

If you showed up, Carol gave piano lessons Saturday afternoons. She knew how busy kids were these days, she said, but she always stayed in on Saturdays in case one of her students showed. She stayed in and baked cookies. She gave lessons on a first-come, first-served basis.

Some kids came just for the cookies. She was famous for her macadamia nut ones. I guess I went that day because I needed to be around somebody who knew me and my family from a safe distance. Somebody who was sane. Carol fit the bill.

Of course, what I should have been doing, as a proper descendant of Lady Sybil of Bernshaw Tower, was practicing some spells. I should have been doing the Peaceful Home Spell. All I needed was a blue candle, tranquility oil, and sandalwood incense. Or maybe I should have summoned Cerridwen, the Celtic mother goddess of the moon and grain, for spiritual inspiration, magical knowledge, wisdom, and personal power.

I needed all that. But somehow I needed Carol and her macadamia nut cookies more.

She came to the door, wiping her hands on a towel. "Hi. Come on in. Want a lesson?"

"You got any other takers?"

"No. Everybody's getting ready for Halloween."

"Sure," I said. I smelled the cookies.

"How are things at home?" she asked, taking my jacket.

I shrugged. "I think I'm having a midlife crisis."

"Bad as that, huh? Is everybody upset because of Jimmy's arrest?"

"What do you think? We're all walking around like we've been struck in our foreheads with arrows."

She nodded. "I'm having a late breakfast. Want some?"

I said yes, and in a few minutes she had a complete breakfast in front of me. I ate, starved.

"Mac called this morning," Carol told me. "He said Dexter came to him and wants to go and live with your father."

"Already?"

"Apparently he was out of the house early."

Dex's door had been closed when I left to go to Naomi's. I thought he'd been sleeping. "Wow, I didn't think Dex had the nerve. What's Mac gonna do?"

"Said he's going to leave it up to Dexter."

How like Mac. To throw the ball back in Dexter's court.

She was watching me. "I know there's things you want to talk about. And I want you to regard me as a friend. We've been seeing each other steadily, Mac and I." She sighed and shook her head. "We still love each other. And I think soon I may be more than a teacher for you. I think maybe soon I could be a sister."

I screamed. I jumped in my chair. I behaved like a demented six-year-old. "You're kidding!"

"No." She put her elbows on the table, her chin in her hands, and tears came out of her eyes. "I just love that fool brother of yours," she said.

I got up and went over to hug her.

"But if you want to talk, anytime, it stays with me. I won't drag your secrets to him. I promise."

"Thanks," I said.

"Go finish your breakfast. I'll get you some cookies."

I sat back down again. She poured herself some coffee.

"Now what did you want to talk about?" she asked.

"It was something about Mac. But suppose you don't

know this about him?"

"I know everything about Mac," she said.

"Do you know about the FBI, and why he quit?"

"The child? I've known that for a long time."

"Is it true what Mom told me and Dex, then? That one of the reasons he came home to Glen Laurel was so she could keep me and Dex? Or is it my mom's way of seeing things?"

"Yes, it's true." She gave me a sly glance. "Mac has a weakness," she said.

My ears perked up.

"He wants to save everybody. I think it's because of his past. He fooled around and didn't get his Power in time to help Martha. Then there was the little girl in the FBI. He wants to make up for those failures. That's why he's so protective of you."

It added up.

"And," she said, "it's why he's helping Darla."

"Darla." I stared at her.

"He's been helping Darla," she said. "All along, even before the accident. Trying to get her steered in the right direction. Away from that dancing, and drugs, toward community college. He even asked me to get her teachers from school to tutor her in rehab."

"I thought he was seeing her on the side," I confessed.

"I know." She smiled. "It's part of his helping everybody thing. He should have been a social worker. But mostly, it's innocence he thinks he has to protect, however he perceives it. Be patient with him, Millicent."

"Sure," I said. "But what do you think will happen if Dexter leaves?"

She shook her head. "He's got a whole set of special feelings for Dexter. It'll devastate Mac," she said, "if he leaves."

We ended up just talking, no lesson. She needed to talk, and so did I. Nobody knew yet that she and Mac planned to be married in the spring. I promised I wouldn't tell.

By the time I left, I knew what I was going to use my wish for. So Dex wouldn't leave us. I'd use the darned thing and get rid of it. Live a normal life like everybody else around me. Lie, fake it, break promises. Just be normal.

It was already six-thirty. I had to gather my things and do my shape-shifting. The day hadn't turned out as badly as I expected. Mom was running back and forth from home to the haunted house, too busy to notice if anything was up with me. Dex came in and out and stayed long enough to tell me he'd talked to Mac, who'd given him Dad's telephone number.

He didn't seem so angry anymore. Maybe Mac was right, letting him decide for himself. If he'd held back the telephone number, Dex's anger would have grown. Well, I'd do my wish tonight for Dex, after I finished attending to my business.

Nobody was home when I assembled my equipment: the box of salt, the apple and knife, the four-leaf clover and the special dish to put it in, the four candles and matches.

Around my neck I had the piece of red wool Aunt Melanie had given me last time, strung with six new chestnuts.

I went to a place behind the house. I was wearing my sturdy laced-up brown shoes and brown socks, pants, and sweater.

Quickly, I took some deep breaths, relaxed, visualized, and danced out my sacred space. Then I stood in the middle of it, picked up the salt, and threw some over each shoulder. I peeled the apple. That was tricky, getting the skin off all in one piece.

I put the four squat candles in the dish at my feet. In the middle of them went the four-leaf clover I'd saved. Then I mumbled the spell I'd learned from Aunt Melanie.

I looped the peeled apple skin through the red wool around my neck. There was nobody to hold hands with, so I hoped the magic would work. I closed my eyes and visualized.

I saw myself as the same young doe. I breathed deeply, absorbing every detail about the doe into my being.

"I shall go into a fawn," I whispered, "with joy and respect and such and mickle care for this creature whose shape I beg to take on; and I shall go in the animal spirit's name, aye, and walk among them, and hear their joys and woes, and I'll come home again."

I kept my eyes shut, hearing only my own breathing, concentrating on it. In my mind I saw the door I must go through with the engraving of the deer on it.

I lifted my feet, one at a time, visualizing them as hooves. Then I felt the warmth, as if I'd suddenly put on a warm coat against the night chill.

It was working! I'd done it on my own!

Was it real? I opened my eyes and heard a dog barking in the distance, heard some faint music, heard water rushing somewhere. I remembered to acknowledge that whether this was perception or reality, it didn't matter. If I believed I was a doe, I was one.

Chapter
Twenty-Four

I went directly to the half-finished house. Overhead, a crescent moon was out, and pieces of clouds were fleeing across it. An owl hooted. I smelled fallen leaves, a nearby stream, other deer.

The outline of the half-finished house rose against the still red and purple sky in the west like a child's drawing, straight, clean lines. A flock of geese were flying into that sunset, their honking deep, throaty, a warning.

I knew what they were saying to me. "Go, go, go, time is running out. Now, now, now."

I stopped at the river bend and went over to the tree I'd taken a stethoscope to once and listened. Bump, bump, bump. Sure enough, there was a regular heartbeat. I didn't know if I could hear it because it was Halloween night or because I was now a deer, but it didn't matter.

Then I went to the river's edge to get a drink. I peered in, and saw it! The sunken city! Tiny houses, castles, farms. Oh, I wished I could hear the singing of the maidens who guided the river spirits! I wished I could see the undines! But all that took time, concentration.

Right now I had to find a place to hide and watch the house.

I chose a clump of bushes a bit away, where I'd have a good view. And shortly after I stationed myself, I heard an approaching car. Far away yet, maybe a mile. The darkness was thickening. The car came closer and closer. I smelled the fumes and the dust as the car stopped in front of the house. Doors slammed and I heard people, saw a flashlight, saw the trunk of the car open like a whale's mouth.

Then I smelled Naomi. I knew the perfume she wore. We'd bought it together at the mall.

I saw her looking around as she shone the flashlight, saw her father, a middle-age man with a mustache, wearing a black windbreaker. He looked a bit like the man who'd asked me for directions to the Lubbock place that day, except that guy had no mustache.

"Come on, no stalling," he said. "Get busy."

They went to the stolen stuff and pulled off the canvas. "Hope these damned stereos didn't get ruined in the damp," he said. "Here, just let me get this in the car first." He picked up a heavy box, walked to the car, and put it in the trunk.

I stepped forward, out of the protection of the bushes, and came down on a tree branch. The crack sounded like a shot.

"Who's there?" Naomi said. "Millicent, is that you? If you're there, you'd better leave. My dad's got a gun. And he's sore enough that you're making us move this stuff tonight."

I stood so still, I could hear my heart beating. Then her father came back. "Who you talking to?"

"A deer was over there by those bushes."

"You sure it was a deer?" He grabbed the flashlight from her. The beam searched out the dark, then fell on me.

He gave the flashlight back to Naomi and pulled out his gun. "Focus it out there again," he ordered.

"It's only a deer, Daddy."

"Focus it, I said!"

She did so. And he was aiming the gun right in my direction.

I was paralyzed by the light shining in my eyes. I couldn't move.

"Daddy, don't!" Naomi yelled.

I saw her push him away just as the gun fired. It sounded louder than dynamite. I ran to the back of the bushes.

"What the hell is wrong with you?" I heard him yell. "Can't a guy have a little fun?"

"I just didn't want you to shoot the deer, Daddy."

I heard a slap, heard her cry out. "Now get to work and help me move this stuff," he growled.

After that they got busy, hauling goods back and forth from the house to the car. Naomi was still crying, and I heard her father say if she didn't stop he'd take off his belt then and there.

Then I heard another car, though I knew they couldn't hear it yet.

Within minutes I saw the red and blue lights flashing on top. It sat there for a minute, and against the crazy dancing lights, Naomi and her father stood in amazement.

"Hold it right there. Freeze." Mac stepped out, holding a gun. His voice cut through the night, just the way he sounded when he told me or Dex not to run upstairs, that we had something to talk about.

If Mr. Carlson knew what was good for him, he'd listen. Instead, he dropped a box to the wooden floor and pulled his own gun from his belt again.

For some dizzying moments everybody stood like that, in a regular Halloween tableau. I heard the police radio crackling behind Mac.

"Put it down," Mac said. "Step away from your father, Naomi, now."

I wondered what Mac was thinking. I hoped he wasn't thinking of the little girl held by her own father as a shield. But I knew he was.

God, I prayed, help him.

Then I wondered where Finnian was.

Naomi stepped away.

"Now, drop the gun," Mac ordered. "Set it down and kick it toward me, Carlson."

"What you gonna do, MacCool? Shoot me in front of my daughter?"

"Nobody's gonna shoot anybody," Mac said. "I'm taking you in, Carlson. I know you go around wearing wigs and disguises."

Carlson didn't drop the gun. "Know where I've been living?"

"If I did, I'd have been there," Mac said.

"Right under your nose, MacCool. At your aunt's bed-and-breakfast. Nice lady, your aunt. I like her spinach quiche."

Aunt Melanie's! So this was the guy who came in with all the packages, who loved her food, who was so handsome!

"The gun! On the ground! Now!" Mac barked in tones he'd never had to use with me and Dexter, because we knew never to bring him that far.

But Carlson had his feet firmly planted apart and wouldn't comply.

Holding the gun steady, Mac spoke into the radio he wore,

calling for backup. "If you shoot, I'll return fire," he told Carlson.

For a fraction of a second Mr. Carlson glanced at Naomi.

"Daddy," she whimpered, "please, Daddy, listen to him. I don't want you to get hurt."

"Shut up!" he yelled.

She shut up.

I should do something, I thought, cause a distraction, make noise so Mac could get charge of the situation. Then I realized it could work against Mac, too, and stayed still.

"I'm gonna count to three," Mac told him. "I expect you to drop the gun by then, Carlson."

"And if I don't? You gonna shoot, MacCool? I've got my daughter here." He reached out, grabbed Naomi and drew her closer to him. "You gonna let her get shot, like you did with that other kid?"

Oh, that was so rotten! I hoped it wouldn't affect Mac, distract him. It didn't.

He stood firm, unflinching. He hadn't even put on a jacket against the night's chill. All he wore was that white shirt that was like an emblem in the dark. His arms were outstretched as he held the gun firm in two hands, his narrow hips steady, his feet solid on the ground.

I felt a rush of love for him. The gold stripe on his pants was like a sword at his side. I wanted the red and blue lights of his car to be a ring of invisibility, as Sir Owain had once had.

But I knew better. I knew that the alchemy for disaster was here. As were all the primal symbols of darkness, of the underworld.

I felt the love emanate from me toward Mac, a warm glow, protective. But it wasn't enough. More was needed.

So I decided. I'd use my wish now. For Mac. I'd save him. But I couldn't. I was too scared, distracted. I couldn't focus my positive energies. I needed to concentrate, relax, breathe deeply, visualize, meditate. And I couldn't do it. Fear for Mac dominated my whole being. And fear is a negative force.

I heard Mac counting. "One . . ." he said.

Then Naomi made a move, this way and that.

It was enough to disturb the delicate balance of the universe at that moment, enough to tip the scales of the cosmos that balanced out good and evil. From somewhere, I heard ethereal music. And the clashing of swords.

"Two . . . " Mac said.

Naomi bent her knees and knelt briefly. She was out of the range of light now. I couldn't see her. So then, neither could Mac. Would he chance it? Chance hitting her? That's what she was counting on, that he wouldn't.

He never said "Three."

Mr. Carlson fired.

"No!" I screamed. But either no scream came out or nobody paid mind.

Everything happened at once then. The bullet from Mr. Carlson's gun missed, went over the hood of Mac's car. Mac ducked behind the open door of the car. And Mr. Carlson took aim again.

Mac returned fire.

He fired low, I saw it, probably to hit Mr. Carlson in the leg and incapacitate him, like he told Dexter and me he'd been trained to do. But Mr. Carlson dropped to the ground in that instant and I heard an "oomph."

Then Naomi screamed. "Daddy! You killed my daddy!"

It ripped apart the silence of the night. Behind me in the woods I heard the animals chattering. "Run, run, they're killing each other again, the fools!"

I saw Mac lower his gun and go to Mr. Carlson. But before he got there, Naomi did. I saw her pick her father's gun from his hand and run with it, out of the house and into the darkness.

"You killed my daddy!" I heard her screaming as she ran. "And he didn't even have a gun!"

Chapter
Twenty-Five

I ran after Naomi. Oh, please, I prayed, I must find her. I must speak to her.

I knew where she was going, to the bend in the river, to the ledge of rock where Martha had drowned, where we'd spent so many nice afternoons together, she and I.

I got there just in time to see her throw the gun in the river. Right where the sunken city was. Then she sat down on the rock ledge sobbing, her flashlight in her hand.

I knew I was my old self again, because I shivered in the night air. I felt the dampness rising from the river.

"Don't you come near me," she said. "Your stupid brother killed my father."

"He fired at my brother first. I saw it."

"He killed him," she said again. "My father never fired a gun. He never had one."

I drew in my breath. So this was the way it was going to be, then. "You threw the gun in the river. I saw you."

She looked at me. She shined the flashlight at me. "You weren't there. You didn't see anything."

"I was at the house, as a deer. You saw me. You kept your

father from killing me."

"I stopped my father from killing a deer."

I felt as if I'd been hit in the chest. Had she seen me as a deer? Had I really been one? Or was she lying now, to trip me up?

She smiled, through her tears. "A deer. And I'm going to tell them. And if you say you saw this as a deer, won't that sound great. People will know then that all you MacCools are crazy."

"I know what I saw," I insisted.

"If you tell them you saw as a person, you'll be lying," she said.

I walked in an arc around the place where I'd left Mac. Police cars were there, an ambulance. There were lights flashing all over the place, radios crackling in the night. Mac would be all right, for now. He'd do the right thing. I had to find Mom and tell her what had happened.

I walked home through the deepening chill. I went right up to the haunted house, cut past the lines of people waiting to get in, past Dennis, who was taking tickets. In the main room downstairs I saw Dex gathering a group around, getting ready to take them on a tour.

He saw me in my regular clothes and scowled.

"Where's Mom?" I asked.

"Upstairs."

I walked right through the hanging cobwebs, into the hall past the mummy. I kicked aside some make-believe bones and rubber snakes on the floor, brushed aside the hanging witch, and went to where Aunt Mercy was playing Celtic music on the harp.

"Why, Millicent, where's your costume?" she asked.

"I need my mom."

"What's wrong, darling?"

"Trouble. I've got trouble."

She stopped playing and came to me. She was wearing something loose with wide sleeves, and she had a band around her forehead. "What kind of trouble?"

Her eyes were so kind. "Aunt Mercy, I shape-shifted tonight."

Her eyes sharpened. "On your own? And you had trouble?"

"Not with the shape-shifting, no. I saw something I wasn't supposed to see."

"Oh, dear." She led me to the stairs, her arm around me. "Go find your mom. She'll know what to do. And tell me later."

Upstairs, the hall was made to look like a cavern. The senior art class had done a good job of it. I found Mom in a room hung with bats and cobwebs, lighted only by candles. She was sitting by a coffin. I shivered, seeing it. Maddie was fixing her makeup.

"Oh, Millicent, here you are," Mom said. "Where's your costume, darling?"

Maddie said to me, "The water Aunt Mercy made is selling like crazy."

"Great," I told her.

But Mom was looking at me. "What's wrong, Millicent?" she asked.

Mom left Maddie and the aunts in charge. By now Aunt Melanie knew that I'd done some shape-shifting, and when I passed her in the hall on the way out she took me by the shoulders. "You really did it? On your own?"

I said yes.

"I don't know whether to spank you or hug you. What happened?"

I leaned my head on her bosom. "I saw Mac shoot somebody." I whispered it low, so only she could hear.

"My God!" She raised my chin with her hand. "Is he all right?"

"Yes."

"Was it justified?"

"Yes."

She kissed my forehead. "Your aunt Mercy and I will be over as soon as we can."

Nobody heard this exchange. I went out with Mom. "Give her one of those powders, too, Mehitable," Aunt Melanie said.

I made Mom go by the police station. She didn't want to, but she indulged me. On the way, I told her what had happened. All kinds of cars were outside the station. Cars I hadn't seen before.

"Outsiders," Mom said. "Outsiders in Glen Laurel. Men who don't know this town. They'll want to take over now. Everything will change."

"No," I said.

"Shooting someone dead requires an investigation," Mom reminded me.

"Mac will be all right, Mom." And then I told her why, what I'd seen, and how Naomi had thrown the gun in the river. "So I can help, Mom. I can tell the authorities what I saw."

"Say that you were there as a deer?"

"No. Just that I was there," I said.

She took her hand off the wheel, reached out and grabbed mine, and held it.

"And I'm going to tell Mac I was there. As a person. And I want you and the aunts to back me up, please."

Inside, Mom put on coffee. "It's going to be a long night. The aunts will be here soon."

I'd started to shake. She gave me one of the powders Aunt Melanie had suggested, and some hot tea and a sandwich.

The haunted house didn't close until midnight, but the aunts came before eleven. Dennis, Maddie, and Dex stayed.

The aunts entered in a flurry of excitement, hovering over me like butterflies in their costumes. One sat on either side of me on the couch.

"You dear child, why didn't you come to us?" Aunt Mercy asked. "The thought of you doing it all on your own breaks my heart!"

I told them the whole story. "It was my fault the stolen stuff was in the house," I finished. "I shared the place with Naomi."

"She betrayed you," Aunt Melanie said. "Don't blame yourself for that."

I looked at my aunts, each in turn. "I should have told Mac about the stuff right away."

"And break your blood promise?" Aunt Melanie asked.

"Are you supposed to keep a promise to somebody who is doing wrong?"

Both aunts looked at each other. Aunt Melanie hesitated. "Mercy, this child has a question for us."

"I know." Aunt Mercy sighed, then looked at Mom.

"Mehitable?"

"I depend on you two. You're the experts," Mom said.

"We must have a conference," Aunt Mercy said. "We must go to our books. We must look up the wisdom of the ancients."

Then she had a thought. "But what did you hope to accomplish there tonight, child?"

"I wanted to move into what I feared. I wanted to face my life in its entirety and discover if all my difficulties were only because of my own stupidities and inner turmoil."

"Dear God!" Aunt Mercy blurted out. "You're too young for that! You don't have enough stupidities and inner turmoil to confront!"

"Yes, I do," I said solemnly. "I've messed everything up already. Tonight I wanted to use my wish to save Mac, and I couldn't. I was too scared. I couldn't focus my energies."

They both hugged me, held me. "You poor little thing," Aunt Melanie crooned. "You saw a shooting. Confront this on a realistic level. You're demanding too much of yourself."

"And as far as moving into what you feared," Aunt Mercy said, "that's an exercise most adults with the Power hesitate to do. You're not ready for that!"

"I'm not?"

"No." Aunt Melanie patted my hair, tucked it behind my ear.

"Wait until you hear what she's going to do," Mom said. And then she told them how I was going to tell the authorities I was there as a person.

More looks between the aunts. They sipped their coffee quietly.

"You'll be lying," Aunt Melanie said.

"You'll lose the Power," from Aunt Mercy.

"It'll save Mac," I told them. "It's the only thing to do. Or else he's finished."

"Unless," and Aunt Melanie held up a finger, "unless we can find some loophole in the ancient writings that says it isn't a lie if you do it to save one you love."

"Lying is lying," Aunt Mercy insisted.

More coffee sipping.

"Anyway," Aunt Mercy added, "it'll take us weeks to go through the writings of the ancients to sort this out. And Millicent doesn't have weeks."

"I'm doing it anyway," I said. "You can't stop me."

"Darling," Aunt Melanie said, "we haven't the right. It's a decision you have to make. But there are things we can do."

"What?" I asked.

They both set their cups down on the coffee table. "We can do a spell for Mac's protection. Right now. And then we can get him a lawyer. A good lawyer. We can't have outsiders running our police department. Mehitable, you have the dragon's blood ink, don't you?"

Mom fetched it from her studio, along with some parchment. Then Aunt Melanie took one of the Halloween candles out of a tin holder and replaced it with a black one.

She wrote what troubles we wished to be rid of, with the dragon's blood ink on the parchment. And our good wish for Mac. All read it and approved. Then she crumbled up the paper and held it over the black burning candle, and we all concentrated on what we wanted for Mac.

"Written wish and burning flame," Aunt Melanie chanted, "let thy powers interweave; grant the wish that we proclaim, on this most enchanted eve. Our secret wish is . . ."

And we all recited what had been on the parchment. Then ended with "so mote it be."

No sooner had we finished than the phone rang, a shrill, cutting sound in the house. We stared at each other. Mom jumped up to answer it.

It was Mac. The aunts were jumping around with excitement, hugging each other and me. Mom shushed them, and we listened as she spoke to him. It was all "Yes, darling" and "No, darling."

Then she said the words I was waiting for. "You have something going for you. Somebody saw what happened."

And she handed the phone to me.

"What the hell were you doing there?" he asked.

I was almost glad to hear the scolding voice. It meant he was okay. I told him.

"Jeez, I wish you'd come to me before this," he said.

"I do, too, Mac. I'm sorry."

"You kids are going to drive me crazy, you know that?"

I said I knew it.

"Yeah, well, you say you saw her toss the gun?"

"Yes. In the river."

"Jeez." His voice was tired. "Okay, that's good. Not that you were there, but, oh hell, I'll call tomorrow. Even these suits who are questioning me have to go to bed sometime. Look, if you say you were there, they'll question you. It'll be rough. They'll ask personal stuff, what our relationship is, and why. It'll come out about Dad leaving. Everything."

"I can handle it," I said.

He laughed. "I know you can. I almost feel sorry for these guys if they question you."

Aunt Melanie got on the phone then. She had a lawyer

friend. She'd call him tonight. He'd be here tomorrow.

Mac must have asked her how she could get him on such short notice. "I have a past, Mac," I heard her say. "Just because I'm in my fifties doesn't mean I haven't."

Chapter
Twenty-Six

It rained all Sunday, heavy, chilling November rain. Day of the Dead rain, with leaves fluttering to the ground all around us. The trees were half stripped already.

I was just finishing dressing to go to Mac's apartment and meet with his lawyer when Dex came to my room.

"Can you help him?" he asked.

"Yes," I said.

"Why didn't you ask me to go there with you last night?"

"It was something I had to do on my own, Dex."

"Were you really a deer?"

"Naomi says so."

"She could be just saying it to make you lie."

"It doesn't matter. I thought I was one."

"If the pistol can't be found, he'll be ruined. They'll take us away from him if that happens."

"I thought you wanted that, Dex. Didn't you ask to go and live with Dad?"

"No. I never made the call."

"Why not?"

"I wanna stay. There's people I care about here. Look, I

knew about the stuff in the house, too. You can tell Mac. If there's any flak, I'll take my share. Tell him that, too."

"Sure," I said.

He turned to go. "You know that Finnian hurt his paw."

"What?"

"Yeah. He cut it on some glass on the job. Otherwise Mac would have had him with him last night."

I wondered how things would have turned out if Finnian had been there. Maybe Mr. Carlson wouldn't be dead. Then I thought about the delicate balance of good and evil Aunt Melanie said our town had. And wondered how last night's events figured into it.

Aunt Melanie called before I left. "This lawyer is the best," she said. "Still, don't talk to him about magic. Keep it low-key."

All Mac said was "Tell the truth."

Mr. Kennerly, the lawyer, was in his fifties. He said he had a daughter near my age. I told him what had happened.

It wasn't as bad as I expected. Mac stayed with me the whole time, and if I lost my Power for lying, I didn't feel any different afterward. And I got to give Finnian some treats and tell him how sorry I was about his paw.

The local paper carried the full story on Monday. There were pictures of Mr. Carlson. It listed the recovered items and gave an account of Mac's background.

Mr. Carlson was part of a ring of thieves that worked small towns. It told how I claimed to see Naomi throw the gun in the river. I saw my name in the paper and it scared me. It was all so final, so *there*. I knew this was what Mac meant when he advised me to reject my Power. I heard him saying, "It's gonna get worse before it gets better." And, "It's a curse, Millicent."

And I thought that maybe he was right.

If they found the gun, the hearing was to be at the end of the week. If they didn't, Mac would go on trial.

I went to the river with the divers the day the newspaper story appeared, to help retrieve Mac's gun.

I took the divers to my rock ledge, the place where Martha had fallen in. "Look in the middle of the river," I said.

The men, three of them, scowled at me. "Why?"

How could I tell them why? Because my sister Martha's spirit was here? And because she'd see to it that the undines would get the gun and keep it? Protect it? Maybe even offer it up to them when they were looking?

Wouldn't that sound great?

"Because she really threw it far," I said.

The police found the bullet Mr. Carlson had fired that missed Mac. I showed them about where Mac's car had been.

I had to give them their due. They were good. They wore plastic gloves and put everything they found in plastic bags. It was just like TV.

By late that day they found the gun. Exactly where I'd told them to look. We all breathed a sigh of relief. Now we wouldn't have to worry about a trial, only a hearing.

Naomi's father was buried the next day, Tuesday.

Our whole family went to the funeral. I watched as Mac went over to Mrs. Carlson to offer his condolences. She turned her face from him. She refused to take his hand. Darla was nearby in a wheelchair, and she took Mac's hand.

Naomi's hair color was different. It was no longer limp and dirty brown, but a soft honey color now. Her skirt came to her knees, black. Her jacket was smart and sharp. She wore a neat white blouse and a black beret. It all looked expensive.

Television reporters hovered in the background. The story had been picked up by the wire services and appeared in daily newspapers around the country.

ROBBER'S GUN FOUND IN RIVER. EX-FBI HERO POLICE CHIEF DIDN'T SHOOT AN UNARMED MAN.

The whole thing was a nightmare.

Even though the gun was found, the hearing was still to go on. And Mac was glad about it. He wanted no question marks after his name.

Dex sat out in the hall with me, on the bench, waiting, while Naomi testified.

"She's gonna tell them that Mac fired first," I said.

"It won't work," Dex assured me. "They've got Mac's gun, with only one bullet fired. If he fired first, he'd have had to fire two, in order to kill her father."

"She'll tell them I wasn't there, Dex. That all she saw was a deer. She'll say I wasn't there."

"Then how could you have told them the gun was in the river?" he asked.

He was logical and calm, a lot like Mac. He kept me from falling apart until they called me.

When they finally did call me, I felt as if I was having an out-of-body experience. I felt myself floating up above it all, looking down on everybody, myself included.

Then, at the last minute, the door of the courtroom opened and a man came in.

It was my dad. My heart lurched inside me. He wore a blue blazer and gray slacks, and he was very tanned. He caught my eye and winked at me. I saw Dex turn, saw his mouth go into a firm, unyielding line. Dad nodded to a few people, then took a seat in the back, alone.

I felt his gaze on me. It took all I could do to keep from looking at him. And I wondered what Mom was feeling.

The lawyer asked me a question. "Why did you go there that night?"

"Because I'd warned Naomi to have her father move the stolen stuff, or I'd tell my brother in the morning."

"Are you close to your brother?"

"Yessir."

"They why didn't you tell him about the stolen goods before then?"

"Because Dex—my other brother—and I were mad at him. For waiting until Dex's friend was eighteen before arresting him. And because Naomi was my friend and I didn't want her to get in trouble."

"Didn't you think your brother, MacKenzie, would be angry with you for not informing him?"

"Yessir. I knew he'd be. I figured he'd be really sore."

"And you still didn't tell him?"

"No sir. I just wanted Naomi to get the stuff out of there. I wasn't thinking clearly. But I went there to make sure they did move the stuff. I was going to tell Mac next morning if they didn't. Honest. I know I did wrong. My brother's been good to me. And I'm sorry."

"Tell us what you saw, Millicent."

I told him. "I saw my brother pull up in his police car and get out and tell Mr. Carlson to hold it right there."

"Did your brother have his gun out?"

"Yes. But Mr. Carlson took his gun out, too. Then Mac told Mr. Carlson to put his gun down. He told Naomi to move away from her father. Mr. Carlson just asked Mac if he was going to shoot him in front of his daughter."

"Then what happened, Millicent?"

"Mac said, 'Nobody's gonna shoot anybody.' And he told Mr. Carlson how the police had been watching him and knew who he was, even with all his disguises. And he told him again to put the gun on the ground. And I thought, I'd do it if I were Mr. Carlson. But he didn't do it. Then my brother called for backup, and told Mr. Carlson that if he shot, he'd return fire."

"So he warned him."

"Yessir. Then Mac said he was going to count to three, and Mr. Carlson should put his gun down."

"And did he?"

"I only heard two. Then Mr. Carlson shot at Mac. The bullet missed. Mac went behind his car door. Mr. Carlson was getting ready to shoot again. I saw Mac aim low and shoot. But Mr. Carlson dropped to the ground, and then . . . then . . ." I stopped.

"Take your time," the lawyer said.

"Then Naomi ran to her father and screamed that Mac had killed him. And picked up his gun. And ran with it. To the river. I saw her throw it in."

I looked up at the faces in the courtroom, all people I knew. "That's what I saw," I said.

I don't know about these things. About the legalities and all. A man in a blue suit cross-examined me. The first words out of his mouth were:

"Why do you live with your brother MacKenzie?"

"I don't. I live with my mom."

"All right, Millicent. But isn't your older brother in charge of you and your twin brother, Dexter?"

Mac had told me they'd get to this sooner or later. I said yes. He asked why. So I had to say it.

"Because my dad left."

He said he'd heard talk around town how I had everything. Was my brother good to me, then?

"Yessir."

"Would you lie for him?" he asked.

I said no. "I don't lie."

He said he heard I had hundred-dollar sneakers. And a pug dog that cost a thousand dollars. Why would I want to ruin something like that? Why wouldn't I lie to protect it?

"My dad sends the money for our keep," I told him. "My brother doesn't have that kind of money. And the dog was given to us by the pet shop because they couldn't sell her, because she was defective."

"I understand that your brother Dexter wants to go and live with your father," he said. "Why? Does Mac mistreat you two?"

Where did these people get this stuff? "No," I said.

"Does he listen and reason? Or does he have a short fuse?"

"He listens," I said. "He lets you explain, argue with him even. Sometimes he just has these dumb rules."

"Like what?" he asked.

I hesitated. "Well, he won't let me wear shorts to the mall."

Laughter, quickly stifled.

"And," I went on, "he gets all bent out of shape if we sass Mom. That's the biggest thing. We can sass him, but not Mom. But no, basically he's okay. He's good to us."

"Then why does your brother want to go and live with your father?" he pushed.

"You should really ask Dex," I said. "But as it turns out, he isn't going to live with my dad. He never even asked. He's staying right here. That's what he told me."

They did call Dexter in, after me. And they went at him with questions about Mac, how he treated us, did he ever hit us, did he have a quick temper. And why had Dex wanted to leave?

Whatever they were looking for about Mac, they didn't find. Without even hearing what I had to say, Dex said much the same thing about Mac as I did.

He was good to us. What else could we say?

Chapter
Twenty-Seven

Again, I don't understand the legal stuff. To me, all the talk between the judge and the blue-suit man and Mr. Kennerly was like a medieval spell they were casting.

They spoke a language of their own and left everybody else out of it. They used all the secrets, clever tactics, charming personalities, wrath, fears, and curses that are in that book of mythology I had to study.

In the end I did understand, though, that Mac was cleared of all charges. His shield, sword, and armor were returned to him.

We left the court with everybody congratulating Mac. He was embarrassed, I could tell. And then, while we were standing on the front steps, Dex nudged me. "Look."

I did. Mom and Dad were off to the side, talking. They approached us. Dad shook Mac's hand, then looked at me and Dexter.

"You two were pretty good in there," he said.

He was his usual charming self. But somehow I wasn't as thrilled this time to see him, not as drawn to him. All I could think of was, He'll put Mom in a state, coming here like this.

I'd seen the look on her face in court. And now. All confused and torn.

He feigned a punch at Dexter. "So, you don't wanna leave, huh?"

Dex blushed. "No sir."

"How 'bout I take these two kids, their mother, and you out to supper tonight?" he asked Mac.

"I have to work," Mac said. "But you all go. Only you two," he looked at me and Dex, "have to go to school this afternoon."

We both protested. But Mac only said, "Get in the car."

Dad put his arm around me and grinned. "Sure you wanna stay with him?" he asked us.

"Yes," I said firmly. And I meant it. It had only been a couple of months ago when he came to see me at the hospital, and I cried when he left. I knew I wouldn't cry this time. I was just glad everything was over, glad Mac was all right, and worried about Mom.

Maybe, I thought, I've moved into what I feared, and faced my life in its entirety, after all.

Mom kissed me. "Will you be okay?" I whispered.

"I'll be fine. Go."

Dex and I made for Mac's car. Out of the corner of my eye I saw Dad put his hand on Mac's arm and detain him a minute.

"I'd give an eye to have those kids talk about me in court the way they talked about you. They are two beautiful youngsters," I heard him say.

"There's room for improvement with them," Mac answered. "I'm working on it."

Then, in the car, something didn't seem right. It was like

when you come out of the dark movie theater on a bright day. Everything was off kilter. Right off, I was getting bad vibes from Mac. He was brooding. I think his body temperature must have dropped four or five degrees, like some shamans could do when they did magic rituals.

At first he didn't talk to us at all. Then when we got out on the Old Stage Road, he did. "I wanna thank you guys for what you did," he said. "And I'm sorry the family's dirty laundry had to be aired like that."

"It's not as dirty as some," Dex said.

Mac didn't soften. "Yeah, well I've always told you both, how we have an image to keep up in this town."

Dex and I didn't answer. It was one of those moments when we were tuned in to each other. We just waited. But Mac didn't speak again until we pulled up in front of the school. Then he cut the motor and just sat there for a while. "We're gonna have to talk about this business of you kids not telling me the stolen goods were in the house," he said.

Still, neither Dex nor I said anything.

"If either of you is ticked off at me for something, you come and tell me. I thought we had an agreement. We get things out in the open, we don't let them fester. We don't plan revenge. We air things out, thrash them out if necessary, and go on. You don't get back at me like that. It didn't look so good."

A bell rang in school. "It's fourth period," Dex said.

Mac slapped the wheel with his hand. "I told you both. You can talk to me anytime! Am I that bad to talk to? You said it out in court. Under oath. I'm good to you. I don't mistreat you. Maybe I should start."

Jeez, he was registering a nine on the Richter scale.

Dex was in the front. I was in the back. Dex turned and slid me a sideways glance. Then he said, "Sorry, Mac, it won't happen again."

I saw Mac's eyes glaring at me in the rearview mirror. So I said it, too.

He sat there for a few more seconds, shoulders hunched. "We're not out of the woods yet, you know. They're going to have a hearing because Naomi admitted to helping her father steal. The kid may be put in the hands of juvenile authorities."

I looked at Dexter and he at me. "Mac . . . " I said.

"You know that her mother could get mad enough to say you two were accessories. We're sitting ducks right now."

"Mac . . . " I said again.

"Yeah, what?"

"There's something you should know."

"Oh, God," he said.

So I told him. How Naomi's father beat her to make her steal. And that's why, a week later, I found myself in another room, with a lady from Juvenile, in a blue suit, who looked at me and said: "Naomi told me that she kept her father from killing you. Is that true?"

"Yes," I said. "He wanted to shoot me."

She made some notes, then looked at me in a queer way. "You seem like a nice, straightforward, put-together young lady. Can you tell me something to help me understand Naomi?"

"Sure," I said.

"When I asked her why her father should want to shoot you that night, she said he would never shoot a young girl.

That you were a deer. I know Naomi's got a bad home life, but does she fantasize often?"

I knew I was moving into dangerous territory here. "No," I said.

"Is it true she runs around in her mother's old wedding gown?"

That wasn't going to look so good for Naomi. But still, I couldn't lie. Not because I still might have my Power, or because the aunts were still studying the ancients to find out. But because it wouldn't be right to lie. Naomi needed the truth right now.

"Yes," I said. "It's true. She said she does it to make a statement about her parents' ragged, failed marriage. The gown is all torn and discolored and ragged."

She nodded. More notes. Then. "This business about the deer. Were you and she pretending? She said you could do magic and turn yourself into a deer."

"Maybe that's the way she saw me that night," I said.

"She told you her father beat her?"

"Yes. I saw the scars on her legs. He beat her to make her help him steal."

She scribbled some more.

"Is she going to be all right?" I asked.

All she would say was yes. Then we were finished. She walked out with me into the hall, where Mac was waiting.

"Could I speak to you alone?" she asked him.

"Sure," Mac said. "Go on out to the car, Millicent."

He never said a word to me later, when he was finished with the lady from Juvenile. But he did give me kind of a look when he got in the car, half surprised, half bewildered.

"What's wrong?" I asked.

"Nothing. I'm starved. What do you think Mom has for supper?" And he drove me home.

I know that sometimes planets appear to go backward, to be in retrograde. But they don't really. It's all an illusion, created by earth.

I know this illusion can affect reality, that there are many illusions that can do so. If you believe something, then you can make it your reality.

I still don't know if I lost my Power.

I'm not sure I still want it, if I have it.

Aunt Mercy says that if I do, I should immediately use it for the good of mankind. I thought that's what I'd already done. Because, in the end, lying to save Mac by implying I was there as a person that night was the same as using it to save him, wasn't it?

But I'm all right with all of it, really. Because, whether I have my Power or not, I know I've faced my life, up to now, in its entirety. Aunt Melanie says that was a big move on my part. I feel good about that alone.

Naomi was going to be all right. She was put on probation, with regular visits from the social worker to the Carlson home. And she was to receive professional counseling. And if there were any more incidents of misbehavior, the judge would put her in a foster home.

She doesn't wear the wedding gown anymore. In school we've drifted apart. She wants nothing to do with me. She never gave me the chance to decide what I wanted. Maybe it's better this way. It's hard for me to forgive her for what she tried to do to Mac.

Some teachers from school have volunteered to tutor Darla at the rehab home, so she can get into community college.

It was over.

Except for one more thing I had to do.

On the Saturday after I met with the lady from Juvenile, it was very windy and cold. The sky was a bowl of pure blue, not one cloud in it. Everything was bright and clear and shiny.

I left the house before Mom and Dexter were up. I bundled up good. And I took along some dried laurel leaves, barley grain, and my small iron cauldron, wreathed in red wool.

I went to my secret place. The ledge from which Naomi had thrown Mac's gun, from where Martha had fallen in.

I knelt on the cold stone. The wind whipped around me. I knew that first I had to get rid of my dysfunctional thoughts.

I sat for a while and meditated. Then I decided to try and light the dry laurel leaves in the bowl.

I had come to thank the spirit of Martha, and the undines, for saving Mac's gun. For delivering it up to the divers.

I tried to light the laurel leaves in the bowl, using the waterproof matches Mom had given me when I got my Power.

I couldn't do it. Every time I struck a match, it went out.

"A great way to start a fire on a windy day," a voice behind me said.

I didn't have to look. I knew it wasn't Smokey the Bear. I turned. I hadn't heard the car pull up. I'd been too busy meditating.

"Hi, Mac," I said.

"I came over for breakfast, and Mom was worried. Didn't

know where you went."

Dex was with him. "Hey, Millicent, if you'd asked, I'd have come. What are you up to?"

They squatted down on either side of me. "What are you doing?" Mac asked. He was grave, attentive, respectful.

Would he give me flak? I told him. "I'm thanking the undines and the spirit of Martha for taking care of the gun so the divers could find it."

He nodded solemnly. "Well, then I should thank them, too, shouldn't I?"

I shrugged. "It's up to you."

"Can I light the match for you?" he asked.

I gave him the matches. He cupped his hands over the small cauldron of leaves, and soon they were lighted. He kept his hands cupped over them until they really glowed. "There you are," he said. "What's next?"

"We have to stand. I hold the bowl and give thanks."

He and Dex both stood, on either side of me. I held up the small cauldron to the perfect blue sky. I thanked the undines. Then I said the little poem I'd written for Martha.

"It's not that I desire to hold the remnants of my sister's soul, but she has lingered at this place to help us. Her spirit I now embrace."

"That's nice," Mac said.

"Now, we've got to throw the ashes into the water," I told him.

They stood quietly while the ashes burned out. Then I scooped them in my hand. "They'll blow back in your face in this wind," Dex said.

"No they won't," I said. "Not if Martha accepts them."

I threw the ashes toward the water. The wind was blowing

in our faces, but the ashes went right against it. And I saw small ripples in the water as they dropped in.

"Martha has accepted them," I said.

"Hey," Dex said. "Neat."

"Yeah, neat," Mac repeated. I could tell he was surprised the ashes had gone against the wind.

We walked then, to his car. He opened the door for me. "Mom's holding breakfast."

I got in front. Dex got in back, then Mac went around his side and got in. As he was leaning toward me to buckle his belt, his eyes caught mine.

"A deer, huh?" he said.

It was the first time he'd mentioned it. "Oh, Mac."

"So you lied."

"I didn't. I was there."

"How? The way you threw the ashes into the wind just now?"

"Does it matter?"

"Yes, it does. If you lied to help me, you lost your Power."

"So what? It was a pain. I'm glad to be rid of it."

"They're not sure, Mac," Dex put in. "The aunts are still studying the matter. Aunt Melanie says there could be a loophole, if you lie to save somebody you love."

Mac put the keys in the ignition, started the car, and, before putting it in reverse, touched the side of my face with his hand. "Good," he said. "That means you still can't lie to me."